Disintegration

LES PENDLETON

Essie Press

Palm Coast Services Inc dba *Essie Press*
901 Sawgrass Court
New Bern, NC 28560
www.essiepress.com
EMAIL: essie-press@lespendleton.com

ISBN for Print: 978-0-9823358-1-9
Ebook: 978-0-982235-8-8

Cover by Damonza

Published in the United States of America
February 2015

This book is dedicated to all the unknown writers of the world. Not those who think they should write a book, but those who have taken the time and given the effort to put their thoughts on paper and have yet to see any rewards for their work. I was there for many years and want them to know it is possible to escape obscurity.

Acknowledgments

Thank you to Betsy Barbeau for her editing work on this novel.

Special thanks to every writer who ever scared the pants off me.

1

"Ah. Mr. Enright, you're awake. I thought you'd be coming around about now. I've been trying to remain close by so you wouldn't come to and wonder what the hell was going on. Being disoriented and waking up in a strange environment can be very confusing. And how are you feeling on this beautiful morning?"

His eyes, still covered with a sticky film, David Enright looked in the direction of the voice that addressed him. "Where am I? Is this a hospital? My head, it hurts like hell. Was I in a wreck?"

"All good questions, David. May I call you David? No, you haven't been in a wreck; no, this isn't a hospital; and your head hurts because you've been anesthetized for the past several hours. That's a very normal reaction, which will pass shortly and…"

"Anesthetized? If I'm not hurt and not in a hospital, why was I knocked out? Where the hell is this place?"

Enright tried to sit up to no avail, finding his body and extremities securely strapped to the gurney he was lying on. After several hard pulls at his restraints, he laid his pounding head back down. "How about telling me why I'm tied to this fucking table?"

Enright's eyes were becoming a little more focused and he could see the features of the man who had been speaking to him. He was short, pumpkin-faced, bald and bespectacled. He was wearing a white physician's lab coat and could easily pass for a member of an emergency room staff. He spoke through a very calming and relaxed smile, very slowly and obviously choosing his words.

"You've been kidnapped, David, by me. You're going to be here with me for quite some time and... Quit pulling at the restraints, please. They're quite strong and you're just going to pull a muscle or abrade your arms. Anyway, as I was saying, you will be here, in my custody, for at least the next few weeks. So, you need to just lie back and relax, get comfortable with your surroundings. Try to..."

Enright yelled as he struggled ever harder with his bonds. "Take these off of me now or you're going to be in a world of shit! I don't give a fuck who put you up to this. I'm going to hold you just as responsible if you don't get over here and release these straps right now. You hear me, don't you? I'm warning you. I'm not just a CPA. I'm also an attorney. Any assault on me is an assault on the court. You don't realize the trouble you're letting yourself in for."

The small frame of his host literally shook with laughter at Enright's threat. He composed himself and continued with his explanations. "It's easy to see how you've become so successful in business, David. You have a very aggressive side to you. You need to forget all of that now and save your attitude for someone else. I have taken every precaution to see that you have absolutely no chance of breaking free. You're not my first 'guest' here and I'm really quite good at rendering one defenseless. I've always been rather small as you can see, so I've learned to use my mind instead of my body. You just relax now. I've got a few preparations to make and I'll be back with you before too long. Oh, and by the way, my name is Kale but I prefer to be called

Doctor K. I'm sure you'll have a lot of things you're going to want to call me during your visit, but Doctor K works for me."

"Is this a ransom deal? That's it? I don't have a lot, of money. I'm married; I've got kids in college and very little cash. You won't get much out of me. I doubt my wife would give you a cent. She'd probably enjoy not paying a ransom for me. You've picked the wrong guy, Kale."

Doctor K offered no response and continued with the tasks he was undertaking in the back of the room. He sorted through vials and other medical accoutrements. Quite preoccupied, he had very little feedback for David Enright. Occasionally, he would correct a point when he apparently found it amusing or so far off base that he deemed it an error worthy of correcting.

"No, David, having studied you for some time now, I would have to agree with you. There's no one who would be willing to pay a ransom for your return. But don't let that bring you to the conclusion that no one is interested in what's going on here. Nothing could be further from the truth. I'm a professional. This lab is not an inexpensive proposition, mind you. My services cost a great deal. I'm very skilled and receiving a tidy sum of money for my contributions to this little affair. As a matter of fact, I've already been paid in full."

"Paid? By who? For what? If this isn't a kidnapping, what is it?"

Doctor K pushed a small stainless steel tray over beside the examination table that Enright was attached to. On its surface was a tray containing a wide array of surgical tools that engendered an immediate response in Enright's facial expression.

"David, I have to tell you; I always love this moment. I'm sure you recognize a number of these wonderful little instruments I have here, don't you? It generally brings to mind many unpleasant childhood visits to the doctor for most folks. I hope you'll forgive me if I take a little too long in explaining this process to you. You must understand how… Let's just say 'involved' I am in this. I get a great deal of satisfaction from what we are about to do here, you and I together."

Enright began testing his restraints again with the same results as before. The only movement that was possible for him was to raise and lower his head. He had seen the bizarre look that washed over Doctor K's face as he spoke and panic was now the most predominant feature on his own.

"I'm not doing a fucking thing with you! You best cut me free this fucking minute. You hear me, asshole?"

"Ah, you're making this so good for me. I knew that you were going to be the best yet. You have so much fire in you. As you can tell, David, I've left you some movement there so that you can watch some of what's going on. I'm sure you will want to, for a while at least. I'm going to have to restrain your head for this first procedure, however. Then I'll give you as much freedom as I can. I actually prefer to have you watch. Now, what do you say we do a few initial 'tests'? I'm very curious as to what your thresholds are."

"You're crazy. Completely fucking crazy! You better not touch me. I mean it, friend!"

Doctor K's eyes danced as he reached into the tray and pulled out a highly polished pair of forceps and a scalpel. "Friend? You're too much, David. Let's see now, these have been thoroughly sanitized, so you don't need to be worried about post-surgical infection. Though that might be very interesting to see. Maybe later."

"Surgery! What are you doing? You fucking moron!"

"Well, David, we are right under my home here and even though I live by myself, I have some very nice neighbors. I don't think they would appreciate hearing these repeated outbursts of profanity that you can't seem to stay away from. And, also, I you may be a screamer."

Doctor K set the two instruments aside and picked up a roll of wide adhesive tape. He pulled off a long section and pushed the middle of it onto Enright's forehead. He pulled on the ends forcing his head down firmly on the table. He then taped the ends to the underside of the table on both sides of his head. Two more, shorter pieces were secured to Enright's lower jaw. With force, he pulled his mouth open wide and firmly taped it in the extreme open position. He smiled as he continued speaking.

"Once, I experienced a very nasty bite from a patient while I was doing the taping. I'm very careful now. They always have more energy during these initial procedures. Can't be too careful. Did you know that a bite from a human is one of the nastiest you can get? The amount of bacteria in a person's mouth is just incredible. I always wear these surgical gloves when I'm working in the mouth. I don't think I could ever have been a dentist. Money might be good, but I'm not doing all that badly here.

"There, I think we're ready. Now, David, I wish I could say, 'I know how much this is going to hurt,' but I can't. I really can't even imagine. However, I'm sure it's got to be a great deal. Pain is such a relative thing and as soon we take care of this little 'quieting' procedure, we're going to get into just what your parameters are. Okay, let's get started now, shall we? You do understand that anesthetics are not a consideration here?"

He looked at the wide-eyed terror in Enright's eyes. "I knew you did."

Doctor K picked up the forceps and scalpel. He first reached in with the forceps, grabbing Enright's tongue firmly. He grabbed and then released it several times before obtaining the hold that he desired. He tightened his grip on the slippery appendage pulling it as far as it would stretch out of Enright's mouth. Continuing to hold it tightly in the extracted position, he picked up the scalpel with his free hand. He held it up so that Enright could see what it was. He twisted the handle in a manner that caused the bright overhead light to flash off the blade creating a sparkle as if it were jewelry. With very exaggerated movements, almost as if he were a magician entrancing an audience, he lowered it to the base of the tongue. He gently probed several times, bringing tiny red droplets to the surface with each touch. Enright's body jumped against the restraints with each touch of the blade.

"You know, David, a scalpel is a really wonderful instrument. If it's a new one, and I always use a new one, they are so sharp that you initially don't even feel the cut. Just a little pressure and then of course, the ensuing warm wetness. There, see what I mean?" Enright could feel it just as his demented captor described. He tried to scream but his vocal chords and even his entire throat quickly filled to choking levels with the warm fluid. He recognized the smell and feel instead of the taste. His taste buds were taking the same journey as his tongue. And, even as he tried to grasp in his mind that this was really happening, Doctor K withdrew the long limp mound of flesh that had filled Enright's mouth only seconds before.

"There now, see what I was talking about? Doesn't even hurt at this point, does it? It takes a few seconds for the nerves to catch on to what's happened to them. Well, you're going to be in quite a bit of pain. Oh, you're choking on your blood, aren't you? I've got a little pump right here for taking care of that."

Doctor K stuck a clear plastic tube connected to a pump down Enright's throat to the point it was beyond the bloody stump where his tongue had once been attached. Enright could see the dark red liquid moving upwards in the tube away from his body. He was getting nauseous at the sight of what had been done to him. The pain began to grab hold of his throat. It started as a burning sensation and quickly escalated to a pulse-actuated pounding. The intensity grew and the pulses became closer and closer in an ever increasing crescendo of agony. As blackness covered his vision, the last image that burned in his mind was his inquisitor staring closely into his eyes. Doctor K's eyes sparkled with excitement as he watched Enright lose consciousness.

* * *

"Welcome back, David. How's that throat feeling?" Doctor K paused and then smiled as he forcefully opened Enright's left eye with his thumb and index finger. "Just nod. I've removed the restraints from your head but I'm afraid you're never going to be much of a talker anymore. Just as well. You really had quite a trash-mouth."

Enright realized that he was awake and back in hell. This was no nightmare from which he was awakening. He wished it were. He wished he could just close his eyes and fall back into a coma-like sleep. His mouth felt empty, much like a giant tooth had been pulled leaving an awkward hole. He still had a tube running down his throat and small bubbles of brownish saliva made their way up the clear pipe to a small pump that had undoubtedly kept him from drowning on his own blood while he was out. It was no larger the bright burgundy it had been when it first started to be pumped from his throat. His mouth felt like a huge empty cavern. The apparatus which had enabled him to talk, to feel the inside of his mouth and even swallow was gone. Only pain remained where it had once been connected to his body. He was consumed with rage, trying in vain to force out a scream.

"That feels pretty odd, huh, David? Here, let me get that tube moved over a little for you. The bleeding has pretty much stopped, for now. But, I certainly wouldn't want you to bleed to death on your first day here. I'd say you are ready now to help me explore a few of my personal fantasies, in complete silence, of course. I hate that you passed out so quickly. The procedure for severing your vocal chords was quite interesting. Removing the tongue does not ensure the complete inability to make sounds but, for me, one step without the other is not very fulfilling. You're going to be as quiet as a little church mouse from here on out."

Enright turned his head and followed every movement that Doctor K made. When he heard the familiar sound of stainless steel being dropped into a tray, his heart rate shot up 'til he could feel his pulse pounding against the sore stub in his throat. Before long, he could see the cart being pushed over beside him again with its cargo of glistening medical paraphernalia resting in the tray. He wanted to cry out, to get up, to slaughter this wicked little man who was torturing him. None of those options was available, so he just laid still on the gurney, eyes as wide as silver dollars, waiting for Doctor K's next move.

"You know, David. I've read that the strongest bone in the human body is the femur and believe it or not, thirty pounds of direct pressure will break it. The only reason that doesn't happen to all of us is the extreme amount of support that muscles and ligaments give to our skeleton. Did you know that? Just nod. Well here's what I propose to do. I say we get rid of all that muscle and ligament support and see if that is true. What do you say, David? Now listen, I'd advise you to move around as little as possible. I'm going to try to make nice smooth incisions here so that the bone gets a nice clean separation from all that tissue. If you jump around and flinch continually, I guarantee this will take a lot longer and wear us both out."

Enright almost passed out when he saw Doctor K pick up the scalpel and twist it in his hand, again watching the light reflect off the blade. The first feeling was pressure, much like that on his tongue. Within seconds however, the sharp stinging began to build. He could feel the blade being run up the entire length of his thigh muscle. Intense pain quickly followed and escalated exponentially by the second. Before long, his right leg felt as it were in a sausage grinder up to his hip. Silent screams poured from his empty mouth each time the butcher moved his elbow in another slicing pattern. Even though he could only lay in mute silence, with just his mind screaming, Doctor K began to hum as he directed the stainless steel razor completely around Enright's thigh muscle. After what seemed an eternity, his mind shut down and blackness once again overcame his reasoning. It was the most welcome of sensations.

* * *

The bright light beckoned Enright. He wanted so badly to move toward it. Even in his semiconscious state he felt that freedom and peace waited for him there. This was to be but another cruel joke. As his mind resurfaced into the cell of the demented character who had so excitedly undertaken his mutilation, his heart jumped back to warp speed and he realized that the light was from a high powered quartz surgical lamp, pulled down close to illuminate Doctor K's handiwork.

"Ah, back again. You were out quite a while, David. You didn't miss a thing. Well, that's not completely accurate. You had company. That's right, old friends dropped by to see how you were doing. They said to give you their 'regrets.' They stayed quite a while, hoping you'd come around and they could watch you and me working together. Unfortunately, you just wouldn't wake up and they ran out of time. I wouldn't feel bad, though. I'm sure they'll be back.

"I notice some concern in your eyes, David. You probably think I'm trying to kill you. Is that right? Well, nothing could be farther from the truth. My whole purpose here is to keep you alive and actively participating in this adventure for as long as possible. For me, one of the greatest feelings of satisfaction I get out of my work is seeing just how long this can go on. I know that you're a smart individual though and that you understand that, ultimately, you will not be leaving here alive. I hate that. If it were possible for me to put my patients back together and somehow make them forget they were ever here, I would be thrilled. It would certainly make my job a lot easier. Disposing of the end product of my procedures is quite a tricky business. I am proud to say, though, I have a system in place for that which seems to be working wonderfully.

"And now, we need to get back to work. You remember, we were going to test the tensile breaking point on a femur bone? I have gotten a spot on yours all cleaned of muscle and tendons and I think we're now ready to start adding weights. If you'll pick your head up a little, you might want to take a look at the amount of work that we've already gotten accomplished. If you'll try to fight blacking out so quickly this time, we might get several more tests done today. What do you say to that? Just nod."

2

"Alicia, are you awake dear?"

"Yes, thank God! What a nightmare I was having. I think these calls are bothering me more than I thought."

"He called again yesterday?"

"There were two hang-ups, but it was him."

"How can you tell?"

"He just hangs on, doesn't say a damn thing. I can hear him breathing, not exaggerated or anything like he's playing with himself, though I'm sure he probably is. There's music in the background. Usually it's an instrumental, jazz, like Brubaker or Kurtz. Then, after he's sure that I know it's him, he just hangs up. What kind of kick could he be getting out that?"

"I don't know, baby. There's just a lot of sick people out there, apparently. Just leave the machine on and don't answer until you recognize who's calling you. I'm going to see about getting the calls traced today. I'm getting tired of this shit. I'm sure the police could care less, as long as somebody isn't getting murdered. They'll probably tell me to just report it to the phone company and they'll trace the call. And, if they ever catch the pervert, he'll get a sixty-day suspended sentence and two-hundred-dollar-an-hour therapy for a year at taxpayer's expense. I've got a good mind to hire somebody to track whoever it is myself and then have the shit beat out of him. That's the only thing somebody like that understands, immediate cause and effect."

"And then, they'd send you to prison."

"You're probably right. For violating the poor, mentally disturbed fellow's civil rights. It's a pretty sick world we're living in."

"Don't you worry about me, Aaron. Morris is here all day. I'll be fine. I'll leave the machine on like you said and the perverted creep can just leave a message. You're leaving for the office already? I thought we might have a cup of coffee before you got away this morning."

"Sorry, darling. Board of Directors meets at nine this morning and I'm sure they all expect the chairman to be there. We'll do something this evening. Will you be all right with that?"

Alicia threw back the covers revealing her well-toned, tanned body and walked pointedly over to where her husband Aaron was fingering the Windsor knot on his silk, Christian Dior tie. Though still fumbling with the tie, he watched as her thoroughbred-like steps caused her breasts to bounce in an incredibly delicious manner. She knew the effect she had on Aaron, and smiled as she approached. She was proud of her body and always excited by the look it put on her husband's face. She stood directly in front of him, threw back her thick, shoulder length, auburn hair and slid both hands up to each side of his neck, disrupting his efforts. He could feel the warmth of her body and smell the residue of last night's perfume as she pressed against him.

"If you won't have coffee with me, at least won't you let me squeeze you a little before you rush out to your boring meeting?"

Aaron Goldman dropped his hands from the knot and took his wife in his arms, massaging her silky back sensually as they kissed. "That what you had in mind?"

"It'll do until we have the time to try something better. Promise you won't stay late tonight?"

"I'll try and get home early, beautiful. You know how tough things are right now. I wish we had never gone public. I liked it better when I had no one to answer to."

"I know, baby, but think about all the money we made. Speaking of money, you're not going to be upset with me if I buy a little something at Furman's today, are you?"

"Since when did I ever mind, and since when did you ever buy a little something? Don't you know that the best things in life are free, Alicia?"

"No. Nothing in life is free. You really didn't think it was, did you, my big hairy hunk?"

"No, I didn't. It just sounds nice to say it. I'll try and be home early. 'Bye, darling."

"Later."

Aaron turned and walked out the bedroom of the Georgian mansion that he and Alicia had called home for the past twelve years. As he left the room, Alicia walked over to the full-length, gold-framed Victorian mirror that stood in the far corner of the room. She walked close to her own image, smiled at what she saw in obvious approval of her reflection. She ran her hands behind her head, pushing her thick hair up, exposing her neck to the downward motion of her hands. She continued the sensual slide downward, enjoying the feel of her hands which she moved as if they belonged to her lover.

There was nothing in the way of opulence that couldn't be found within the great home's many rooms. Antique furniture, crystal, and porcelain figurines filled every square foot. More than a few works from the Old Masters hung on the walls. This was not, however, a case of new money being over-displayed for the pure cultivation of yuppie envy. To say the least, the Goldmans represented some of the oldest money in a town known for its collection of ancestral estates and large bank accounts. Their home and possessions seemed only appropriate to those who knew them. They certainly made no excuses for their affluence nor did they throw it in the face of anyone with less, which was just about everyone they knew. As Aaron piloted his vintage E-type Jaguar along the freeway, he hit the top, right, auto-dial button on his car phone. His friend and legal counsel picked up on the second ring.

"Morning, Aaron. You ready for the meeting?"

"How did you know it was me?"

"Who else would call me this early, other than my commander in chief?"

"Hey, pal, you got it easy with me. Four hundred grand a year to keep a bunch of investors happy and away from me. And, as old and worn out as they all are, they should be no match for a silver-tongued, Harvard lawyer such as you."

"Rave on, Aaron. Dealing with Ernest Pearlman is like mowing grass in a minefield. He's always got an agenda other than the one he's arguing about, and that's continual. He's the most contentious old bastard I believe I've ever dealt with."

"Yeah, and he wants my ass!"

"You got that right, but trust me. I can handle him. He keeps telling me that one day he'll have control of the company and I'll be the CEO. Isn't that reassuring coming from your own attorney?"

"Even if you thought he could do it, you know who butters your bread."

"That's a fact, Aaron. You've rewarded me quite handsomely for services rendered and I have no complaints. Okay, enough bullshit. How do you see us handling the foundry situation? You know he doesn't want to spend another penny in upgrading. I put it all on paper last night. You can just argue the figures with him. Productivity and equity are both up and you can confidently assure the board of a good return to the shareholders in spite of the cash outlay. He hasn't got anything to grab hold of, other than to say he just wants more. The majority of the board will side with us. I polled a good cross section of them and you're okay. Just put on your 'what a nice guy I am' face. They'll all kiss your ass and you'll come away happy. Got it?"

"Leave the papers on my desk. I'll be there in about thirty minutes."

"See ya."

* * *

Alicia took her time selecting a suitably stylish ensemble to attend the auction. The dozens of designer originals in her cavernous closet kept her prepared for any function. That accomplished, she sat in front of the lighted mirror and painstakingly applied her makeup. If she could be accused of anything, it was the vanity that often befalls a woman of affluence during her mid-thirties. As new wrinkles appeared, she would spend a disproportionately greater amount of time and money attempting to maintain her looks and physique. There were daily trips to the health club for sessions with her personal trainer as well as frequent appointments at the beauty salon for facials and extensive hair management. Lately, she was contemplating the merits of cosmetic surgery. After an hour or so of carefully applying her makeup she picked up the phone and dialed the in-house intercom.

"Morris, are you there?"

"Yes, Mrs. Goldman. I'm in the kitchen having a coffee. Are you ready?"

"Five minutes, Morris. Let's take the Town Car. It's clean, isn't it? Really clean?"

"Yes, ma'am. Just waxed this week. I'll be waiting out front."

"Thank you, Morris."

A smile endorsing the success of her morning rituals crossed Alicia's face as she walked toward the bedroom door. Halfway across the enormous room, her thoughts were interrupted by the phone. She walked over to the imperial French nightstand that held the answering machine. Her smile disappeared quickly. After three rings, the machine answered. She listened for a familiar voice but none was forthcoming.

"You sick bastard, talk to yourself!"

She returned to the huge armoire and opened the mirrored door. After a few moments of searching, she withdrew a black silk negligee and laid it across the foot of her bed. She was excited about the evening that she and Aaron had planned. Even though he occasionally let her down to respond to the demands of business, for the most part he was dependable, especially when it came to matters pertaining to their bedroom. They had been married for fourteen years but the romance and sexual fervor seemed to be still intact for them. She wondered how so many of her friends stayed married to men for whom they had lost all attraction and respect. Perhaps they had just not taken the time to find the right mate in the first place. She and Aaron, despite some philosophical differences, enjoyed most of the same pleasures and were still good friends as well as lovers. After putting the final touches on her hair and double checking her countenance in the Louis XIV mirror, Alicia went downstairs to the front entrance where Morris stood beside the Bristol black limousine with the door open.

"Morning, Mrs. Goldman."

"Late night, Morris?"

"Why do you ask, ma'am?"

"Morris, I've told you before, I detest the smell of stale whiskey. For God's sake, if you are going to run around all hours with Lord knows who, at least take the time to gargle some mouthwash before you come to work."

"I swear, I…"

"Morris, I don't even want to hear it. Just don't do again."

"Yes, ma'am."

Alicia got into the back seat and Morris shut the door behind her. They had a working relationship, almost a love-hate situation. He would put up with her air of superiority and she would not part with him for the world. It was fine for her to inform Morris of his shortcomings, but she would not tolerate any criticism of him from others. After all, he was her choice.

As he got behind the wheel, Alicia asked, "Do you have the morning paper with you?"

"Yes, ma'am, right here."

He handed it back to Alicia and she scanned the headlines as the limousine proceeded to downtown Richmond.

"Morris, when you were growing up in New York, had the schools already been integrated?"

"New Jersey."

"Beg your pardon?"

"I grew up in New Jersey… Newark, and yes, there were a lot of blacks in school then. Busing started about then and I can remember a lot of people being upset about it."

"I've always lived in Richmond and I can't recall very many problems during that period."

"You went to public schools here?"

"Well no. I…"

"There's your answer. You didn't have to deal with it. Folks with money have all these great ideals they think everybody else should have to live with."

"Well, it doesn't look like any of the efforts to bring the lower classes into the mainstream have paid off, now does it?"

"How's that, Mrs. Goldman?"

"Just read the paper. Almost all of the crimes are committed by blacks and Mexicans."

"That's true. You're exactly right there, but you got to take into consideration that being poor and illiterate doesn't lend itself to mainstreaming into the age of computers. There ain't a lot of IBM handouts in the ghetto."

"Nonetheless, Morris, even if I were dirt poor, which granted I never have been, I still would not resort to robbing people to make money. I wouldn't be too proud to mow lawns or paint houses or anything like that."

"Still wouldn't solve the problem."

"Why is that?"

"A lot of the people who do these things are already making a living mowing lawns and painting. Problem is, they can't make enough money to keep up, send their kids to college or even keep food on the table. Lot of 'em start drinking or taking drugs 'cause they can't deal with it, and there you have it. No easy answers, Mrs. Goldman."

"I see you've thought about this before, Morris."

"Lived it. Well, we're here. More limos than the Super Bowl. I guess being given the opportunity to blow a wad of cash on some dead guy's finger-painting is a lot of fun, huh?"

"Don't be haughty, Morris. If people like me didn't support the arts, there would be no Monets or Van Goghs around today for people to treasure."

"I'll take the Super Bowl, thank you."

"Morris, I'll be two hours at the most. You can go get a cup of coffee and maybe some mouthwash."

"I'll be back in thirty minutes. I'll be waiting in the lot across the street. Just wave."

"I will, and please don't make me wait."

"I'm dependable as rain, Mrs. Goldman."

"My concern, exactly."

Morris doubled-parked and then opened the door for Alicia. She stepped to the curb, put on a pair of dark glasses, even though the day was overcast, and walked to the door of the prestigious auction house.

"Good morning, Mrs. Goldman. I knew you'd be coming." The uniformed doorman had seen Alicia attend the auctions enough times to be somewhat familiar with her.

"I'm not that predictable, am I, Delbert?"

"I knew when I saw them unpacking all those old paintings this week that you'd be here for certain."

"I'm glad I didn't disappoint you. Good to see you again."

"Thank you, Mrs. Goldman. Good luck."

"Luck has nothing to do with what goes on here."

Nodding to acquaintances as she moved effortlessly through the crowd, Alicia found her way to the large double oak doors that opened to the main floor of the auction house. She recognized almost everyone in the gallery. There was an out-of-town broker or two but, for the most part, the patrons were the same group of wealthy collectors that attended every auction where there was a notable work or two being placed on the block. Alicia mingled with the crowd and found her customary position on the third row by the wall. The auctioneer knew her well and when calling for bids on an item he knew she would be interested in, he would never conclude a bid without looking her way. It was widely known that when Alicia was interested in a piece, a bidding war with her would be fruitless. She knew the value of the items she bid on and if you outbid her for them, you would be paying too much. The crowd small talked until the auctioneer took his place at the podium. After running a dozen or so pieces through, a beautiful porcelain Meissen figurine went onto the auction block. Alicia recognized it instantly and after a few lower bidders began to fall by the wayside, she entered the bidding.

"Thirty-two hundred. I have thirty-two; do I hear thirty-five? Thirty five! I have thirty-five; can I get four? Four and now five, five and half, six; do I hear seven?"

The bidding was now down to Alicia and one other bidder. Alicia bid seven thousand. She knew that she was approaching the maximum value of the statue, but she also didn't want to be outbid by this particular patron whom she knew only too well.

"I've got seven; can I get eight? No? I'll take seven and a half; can I get seven and a half? Going once, twice, going... The competitor raised her jewel encrusted hand to her eye.

"Okay, now I've got seven and half; can I get eight?" Alicia smiled and nodded.

"I've got it; the bid is now eight thousand dollars." The auctioneer looked at the other bidder. This time there was no response other than a disgusted glance toward Alicia.

"The Meissen is sold for eight thousand dollars to Mrs. Alicia Goldman. Thank you. Our next item is a series of Dresden figurines."

After another thirty minutes, Alicia, feeling somewhat guilty for paying too high a price for her trophy got up and went to the lobby of the auction hall. As she entered the room and picked up a crystal goblet of champagne from the caterer's table, she saw her recent competitor coming toward her.

"Alicia, I'm sure you know that piece was not worth that much."

"Not to you, Delores, but for me it was a bargain."

"Come now, dear, everyone in the room knew that you were just trying to outdo your big sister."

"I would never spend money just to hurt you, darling. I realized that you were in over your head and didn't want to see you have to suffer for the arts."

"You seem to forget, Alicia. My inheritance was the same as yours."

"That's quite true. You just had the lack of vision to want cash and let me have the company. A very big mistake, darling, but that's always been your shortcoming, your need for immediate gratification and of course, no work."

"I couldn't have control of the company if I'd wanted it. You know our beloved father could not bear the fact that I am a lesbian. He was a primitive, a dinosaur. I was by far more capable in business matters than you and, for that matter, more interested. All you ever cared about was how nice your hair looked and that all the women in your bridge club were jealous of your money and power. Running a business was never in your DNA, darling sister."

"It doesn't have to be 'in my DNA.' I'm married to a man who is extremely capable, interested, and just wants me happy. That's a scenario that you will never be able to relate to, I'm sure."

"Just so you'll know, my broker has tripled my portfolio in the last ten years. I can have just as many toys as you if I want, and I don't have to take care of any little boy's ego in the process."

"Don't waste your time trying to put Aaron down. He doesn't need any endorsements from you or anyone for that matter. Virginia Industrial is doing wonderfully thanks to him. Our father would have loved him, probably more than his two bickering daughters. Do come visit with us when you can, Delores. I really have to run now and find a spot for my new toy."

"I have to say, Alicia, he may be a wonderful man but you are the best day's work he ever did. Oh, and don't keep a light on for me."

The two feuding sisters turned their backs to one another and went their separate ways. Alicia left instructions with the auction house for the delivery of her prize and then left to meet Morris. It had begun raining during the auction and she had no umbrella so Alicia stood in the covered threshold waiting for her driver. After nearly thirty minutes, she disgustedly decided to venture into the rain and over to the parking lot where Morris said he would wait and watch for her. There were a lot of people standing under the canopied entrance, so perhaps he couldn't see her. He should have known she would have been there, though. Her fuse had already been lit by her encounter with Delores and she was fuming by the time she reached the lot. And, there sat the black Lincoln Town Car.

"That slacker," she thought. "If he's been drinking again, he'll be looking for work tomorrow."

Just as she reached the back door of the car, the darkened sky let loose its entire volley of rain and a torrential downpour began to explode on the pavement all around Alicia.

3

Fred Burns was dropping the documents on Aaron's desk as he entered. He was not only the company attorney and Aaron's closest business associate, he was the one Aaron turned to for advice on every level. They had planned the course of the business as well as socialized together for many years.

"Pearlman is out for bear today, Aaron. The best way to handle him is to make it apparent to all of the directors that he's just an old pain in the ass. That's something they can't deny because they know him. It'll be a consider-the-source issue from that point on. His personality is your best weapon. Also, we've been notified that he's asked for an audit of all company records again. I'm going to ask the secretary to back off and deny the request this time. They have never found so much as a penny that's unaccounted for and it costs a fortune to stop everything and produce all the books. I don't think they'll go along with the bastard this time. By the way, how's Alicia? Diane and I still want to go to New York with you this month. She's driving me nuts to go see a show. Okay, that's all; go get 'em champ! I'm just down the hall if you need me."

"You don't want to sit through this with me, huh?"

"People don't trust someone who wants their attorney present when they speak. Sorry, wish I could be there."

"Like hell!"

Aaron hated to meet with the Board of Directors. Sure, they owned stock and had a vested interest in the success or failure of Virginia Industrial. However, their collective knowledge of the intricacies of running a state-of-the-art structural steel manufacturing plant would not get the company through a single day's operation. Every quarter, when this group met, he wished that the company had remained closed, with no outside investors. The money generated by going public had, no doubt, put the company on the map, not to mention the personal wealth it had put in his pockets. They were now traded on the New York Stock Exchange and watched over by the SEC in addition to a host of investor-related auditors.

And then there was Ernest Pearlman. Pearlman was a wealthy industrialist from Connecticut. A longtime associate of Aaron's late father-in-law who had founded the company, Virginia Industrial had been on his mind as a ripe business opportunity ever since Carl Thompson died. He had seen the potential in the company and its undervalued assets. His nose for a good investment had led him to put several million in it during the first public offering. Needless to say, he had made a bundle and secured for himself the position of principle stockholder, alongside the Goldmans. Aaron hated him. Pearlman was disgusting. He was obnoxious, loud, enormously obese, and the stench of his imported cigars stayed with him continually. If that weren't enough, he was smug and self-important. He took credit for much of Aaron's and Virginia Industrial's recent growth and made his opinions a point of contention at every board meeting.

This day had been no exception. After hours of offering company earnings projections, revisions to employee pension plans and health benefits, it was finally time to address a large capital improvement program that Pearlman was dead set against.

He breathed heavily as he spoke, barely pausing enough to keep his huge frame supplied with oxygen. His face grew redder as he spoke.

"I say we keep the foundry area just as it is and save the money. It's been good enough all these years and it's too damned expensive to upgrade. Besides, it would kill my dividend next quarter. My wife's planning some expensive trips and she would be pissed off if I had to tell her we couldn't go." Pearlman grinned at his own remarks and took a big drag from his cigar. He had been told at least a hundred times that smoking was not permitted in the offices but he felt the rules applied to those a little less significant than him.

Aaron countered, "With all due respect to Mrs. Pearlman and her desire to travel, let me add that a lot of the countries you might visit have new foundries and, far cheaper labor than we have here. If we're going to remain competitive in this industry we need to continually upgrade our plant and manufacturing systems. If we don't, these meetings will be very dismal affairs in five years. Trust me on that. I'm bidding against these people all the time and they have pencils with very sharp points. They have also had a tendency to dump steel into the US on a moment's notice if revenues start to fall. Their plants were all built after World War II and they are state-of-the-art. Competing with them is hard enough when they're trying to make a profit. If they start dumping steel, we'll have to match price or lose market share.

"The only way we can lower the price is to lower the cost and that, ladies and gentlemen, requires continual investments in technology. I think we've heard from both sides on this matter now and we need to see how all of you feel. Those in favor of allocating the capital to make these improvements, please raise your hands. Six, seven, good. That's a majority, the issue passes."

Pearlman fumed and stood up again. "Let me tell you something, young man. I did business with your wife's father for over forty years. I know how he would have voted on pissing away our money on things we can do just as well without. This company was built on conservative business sense and you need to show a little more of it. I understand that the majority rules here, and it should, but you all understand that even though our votes all count the same, I have a lot more invested here than most of you. I'm getting close to calling for a general stockholder's meeting and a proxy vote to see if we can't get Carl Thompson's son-in-law here straightened out. That's all I have to say."

Pearlman turned and stormed out of the room. Looking flushed but still composed, Aaron Goldman addressed the shocked room. "1 apologize that you had to put up with this. I'm not looking for a war with Mr. Pearlman. He has forgotten that I have more at stake here than he does, including more stock. My entire career is vested here, not just money I've made elsewhere that I invested. I think you all voted correctly and you will find that the long-term rewards will be greatly improved as a result. On a sad note, I wanted to mention to the board that a long-time employee passed away since our past meeting. David Enright, whom most of you knew, was our comptroller, an attorney and a wonderful person. He died in a boating accident about a month ago. The exhaust blower had apparently failed to come on and the gas fumes caused his boat to ignite when he cut the engine on. He perished in the explosion. It was a real tragedy and I'm sure some of you will want to send condolences to his family.

"Well, unless there is other business, we can adjourn now. There are refreshments in the lounge and any of you that would like to stay over for dinner, I'll be hosting it at the Madison, one of Richmond's finest restaurants if you haven't been there before."

He knew when he made the offer that it would ruin his date with Alicia, but under the circumstances he felt he needed to foster as much goodwill as he could with the board. There were some members who sided with Pearlman and their votes could be critical on future issues. He hated to have to deal with such an asshole on top of the headaches of running the company. Aaron particularly hated when he was compared to his wife's father. They were never close and Pearlman knew it. He had a powerful button to press.

A young employee came up to Aaron as he stood talking to a few of the directors who were taking him up on his offer of an evening meal. "Mr. Goldman."

"Gentlemen, this is Mark Williams, our new administrative assistant up front and quite a whiz on the computer."

"Could I speak to you just a second, sir, alone?"

"Of course, Mark. Gentlemen, excuse me just a moment if you would." He walked into a small, empty office with the young man.

"There's a couple of men in the front lobby wanting to speak with you."

"I'm sorry. I'm taking some of the directors out this evening. Find out what they want and tell them you'll try and get them an appointment for later. Why can't they talk to Burns? He deals with salesmen more than me anyway. Yeah, have them see him."

"Mr. Goldman, they're from the Sheriff's Department. They said they needed to speak with you."

"They didn't say what they wanted?"

"No sir. They just said they had to talk with you on a personal matter."

"Damn. This is the last thing I need right now."

He returned to his guests. "Would you please excuse me for just a few moments? I have a business matter downstairs that requires my presence. I won't be long."

Goldman made his way quickly down the stairs to the impressive lobby. Still standing by the front entrance were two plainclothes officers. They had the standard "we're serious people" look on their faces and glanced toward Aaron in a very analytical manner. He had dealt with people long enough to know when he was being "sized up."

"You gentlemen need to see me? I'm Aaron Goldman."

"Yes, sir. Bob McDermott. I'm a detective with the Henrico County Sheriff's Department and this is Detective Clarence Brown. If we could have a minute of your time, we need to speak with you."

"That's about all the time I have, but I'll be glad to take a moment for you. Let's use this office here." They followed Aaron into a small sales office adjoining the lobby.

"Take a seat if you like. Now, what can I do for you? Not another employee with domestic problems or bad checks is it?"

"No, sir. It's your wife, Alicia Goldman."

"Oh, no! She's not been in a wreck has she? She's all right, isn't she?"

"We don't know, sir. It appears she has been abducted."

"Oh, my God! Kidnapped?"

"That's how it looks to us now, sir."

"What makes you think that?"

"We found a black Lincoln with plates registered in your name, empty, the motor running, in a parking lot downtown. It was in the Shocko Slip area, across the street from that high dollar auction house…"

"Furmans?"

"Yeah, that's the place. Anyhow, like I said, the car was empty. One of our patrol cars came across it when he was making his rounds. The officer checked around the area and found a body stuffed under another car close by."

"Not... Alicia?"

"No, sir. Our best guess is that it's her driver. He had on a uniform."

"Oh no. Not Morris. He's got a wife and kids. Unbelievable. Who could do such a thing?"

"The truth is, Mr. Goldman, a lot of people not only could do it, but actually do kill people every day."

"We asked a few questions and the gentlemen that worked at the auction place, a Mr. Delbert Kinney, said he knew you and that your wife had just been at an auction there that morning. We asked some more questions, put a few facts together and here we are. It looks to us as if the driver was killed and your wife was taken. Whoever did it must have known what car she would be getting into. They did away with the driver, shoved him under a nearby car, and waited in her limo. She gets in, another vehicle is pulled alongside and she's gone. A lot of that is just surmising at this point, but I'd be willing to bet that it's pretty close to what happened. The forensic people are going over the vehicle and the area now. We should know a lot more when they're done. You following all of this?"

"I'm floored! Morris' family... His kids. I don't how I'm going to tell his wife about this."

"You might want to call her, but she already knows. Officers have been in contact with her earlier and asked her to come to the morgue to identify the body."

"That's just horrible! But Alicia... Why in God's name would anybody take Alicia?"

"With all due respect, Mr. Goldman, look around here."

"You mean ransom? They want money?"

"Happens every day. If somebody will knock over a convenience store and kill the clerk for ten bucks, you can just imagine what they'll do for a couple hundred thousand or a million."

"I'll pay. Just find out how much they want and what they want me to do. I want you to get her back as quickly as you can. If they hurt her…"

"We'll try sir. First, someone will have to contact you about a ransom if that's the case. We'll be monitoring the calls, of course, and try and figure out just who's behind this."

"Listen. I don't want to do anything that will jeopardize getting Alicia back safely. If they don't want the police around, that's how it's got to be. I'm not taking chances with my wife's life."

"Actually, this is all a little premature, Mr. Goldman. Right now we need to just assemble all the facts and see what we come up with. Are you all right?"

"Obviously I'm more than a little shook up. I still want to do whatever I can to help. What do you want me to do?"

"First, we'd like to ask you some questions. Maybe you've got a good picture of Mrs. Goldman."

"Of course, I'm sure I do. It would be at the house… No, I've got one on my desk. Tell you what. There's some people upstairs waiting for me. Let me get rid of them. I'll pick up the picture while I'm there and be right back. That okay?"

"Yes, sir. We'll wait here. By the way sir, did I see a coffee pot in that room we passed?"

"Help yourself. I'll be right back."

"Oh, one other thing, Mr. Goldman."

"Yes?"

"You shouldn't discuss this with anyone. At this point, only the authorities, the abductor, and you know what's going on. We don't want this to get spread around. It could hurt the investigation."

"Absolutely! I understand."

The two officers made their way to the small break room and poured themselves a cup of coffee. McDermott looked out the door and down the hall to see if there was anyone within hearing distance. "What's your opinion, Clarence? Seemed genuinely surprised to me."

"The money was hers, right?"

"That's the way I hear it, but the word is they get along fine, never been any problems that have gotten out. My wife's father worked for Mrs. Goldman's father for years. He always loved the place and the family. Couldn't wait to get to work. Jesus, twenty-five years at a friggin' foundry. I'd commit suicide."

"There's a lot of folks that'd say the same about what you do."

"Get off it. Great organization, tremendous co-workers and pay that can't be beat."

"Yeah, and the opportunity to meet a bunch of drug dealers, child molesters, and oh yeah, dig bodies out of trash dumps. That's always been my personal favorite."

"Yeah, mine too."

Aaron stopped in Fred Burn's office on the way to make his apologies to the board members. "Fred. Hate to do this to you, but something has come up and you're going to have to take some of the directors to supper. Be the proper host and make sure they all leave well fed and happy."

"What's up? Trouble at the plant?"

"No, it's family. I'll tell you about it later this evening. Get up with me after you get back tonight."

"Consider them properly entertained."

"Thanks. I'm going to go offer them my apologies and you can take it from there."

"Done. I'll call Diane and be right behind you."

Burns could not help but recognize a look of concern on Aaron's face. "You sure everything's okay? Pearlman didn't shake you up, did he?"

"No, nothing like that. I'll get with you later. Look, just take care of things for me this evening."

"Of course, Aaron."

Goldman went back to where the group of directors was growing impatient. "I hate to do this, but I'm going to have to get Fred Burns to fill in for me. We've had a family crisis and I'm not going to be able to go with you. I will definitely take a rain check for the next meeting."

One of the men in the group spoke up. "Is there anything we can do, Aaron? Is your family all right?"

"Yes, everyone is fine. One of my aunts had a slight stroke and has been asking to for me. My mother's favorite sister, so I'm pretty much obligated to go see her. I'm sure she'll be fine. And, again, thank you for your support today. I'll stay in touch with you all."

Goldman returned quickly to the downstairs office and the waiting officers. "Sorry I took so long. Okay, what do we do first? Nothing will take priority over this until I have Alicia back."

"Would you be able to come down to the Broad Street station with us and meet with the Captain? Maybe forensics will know something by the time we get there."

"I'll follow behind you in my car and stay as long as I can be of benefit to you. Let me ask you honestly, what do you think the chances are of getting my wife back alive?"

"If money is what they're after, they'll keep her alive as long as they haven't got it and they think there's a chance they will. If they feel like we're on to them or that they're not going to get it, that's another matter entirely. That's the reason we have to move fast and find out who we're after. Can you leave now?"

"I'm right behind you."

* * *

Fred Burns was the perfect host. After imparting all the appropriate jokes at just the precise moment, he had the directors who had remained behind for supper literally eating out of his hands. "Goodnight, gentlemen. It has been a wonderful evening and I assure you that no one here had a better time than me. I'll look forward to our continuing these great stories after our next board meeting."

Burns walked the last of the men to the door of the restaurant and then returned to the piano bar for a drink. The bartender knew him well. "Another directors' meeting, Fred?"

"That's right, Mackie. How about a Manhattan? Don't spare the whiskey either."

"Mr. Burns, I'm hurt. You know I never cut my drinks."

"All right, Mackie. I'm just keeping you honest. You don't get to the top in business by taking anything or anyone for granted. I question everything. And, I gotta tell you, I'm doing pretty damned good. By the way, any calls or messages for me this evening?"

Mackie reached under the bar for a slip of paper as he replied, "I'm glad you asked me. It had already slipped my mind. Been a real busy night. A guy gave me this note about an hour back. He said to not come and get you, just give it to you after your meeting."

Burns quickly examined the note, downed his drink in two swallows and made a quick exit. The evening had cooled off and a strong wind pushed fog-encased bursts of cold air under the streetlights. Wrapped up in his heavy topcoat, dodging puddles in his Gucci loafers, he made his way around the parking lot until he located a stretch limo parked among a group of cars in a distant corner. A rear door opened and Burns quickly entered the vehicle, pulling the door to behind him.

"Burns, I see you have sent off the remainder of our board. I trust they had an expensive meal on the company."

"You know Aaron. Nothing but the best for the directors."

Ernest Pearlman took a long drag off his cigar as he spoke. "Yes, Burns. I know Aaron Goldman only too well. I've made quite a study of him, you might say. Aaron is one of those people who has the ability to spend other people's money and not feel even slightly squeamish about it. It's a trait that you generally find among people that never had to spend a day performing any sort of physical labor in their entire life. I'm sure that the closest he ever came to a backache was after a hard afternoon of racquetball."

"Granted, Aaron has led a rather privileged life, but let me assure you, he does put in the hours at the company. Hell, it's hard for me to get a minute to call you when he's not looking right over my shoulder. He knows what's going on, except for our little arrangement, of course."

"I certainly hope so. I've placed a great deal of trust in you, Burns. And about our arrangement, you are making progress?"

"In ninety days, Mr. Pearlman, Aaron Goldman will be one of the most despised men in Virginia. The board will literally divest themselves of his presence. You will step in, of course, and lead the company out of a difficult situation and…"

"And, you will become the new president of Virginia Industrial, Burns, if everything works as you are describing."

"It will. I'm very good at quietly directing things, from behind the scenes. It will happen precisely the way I said. And the stock options... One million shares, right?"

"The minute you take over the company, I will put the motion forward and you will become a very, very wealthy man. I'm not the sort of person who is ever surprised by what money can buy, Burns, but I have to admit that I was a little surprised at how quickly you jumped ship."

"I never saw myself as a permanent, second banana to anyone. Since I wasn't fortunate enough to marry into the company, I have to take my own course. Besides, I believe you and I have a more compatible vision of the future, our future."

"Very true, Burns. I can see you ten years down the road, right now. You're a young man with a big future. Don't let it slip away from you with a screw-up in this matter."

"Every 't' is crossed, Ernest; every one."

"Good, I don't deal well with failure."

* * *

The Broad Street police station's turn-of-the-century exterior, with its warm red brick and decorative concrete trim, lent a deceptive impression of the madhouse that churned inside. Aaron Goldman followed the two officers into the arched entrance and down several hallways until they arrived at a section of antique administrative offices full of gray metal desks and mountains of paperwork in every direction. The walls had posters and missing persons photos stapled on top of each other so profusely that it appeared half the world must be either wanted or missing. The smell of coffee brewing combined with the stench of stale ashtray residues completed the picture of a place that was not only worn out, but still working beyond its intended capacity.

Most of the offices were empty and Goldman could only surmise that any good detective would probably be out pounding the streets this time of day. His impression of the officers accompanying him was not all that good. They were serious and enthusiastic but they just didn't seem that sharp. Were they up to the challenge they faced in finding Alicia safely? Should he hire some sort of private detective to help or maybe even call his contacts in state government to make sure the best people were on this case? He decided to defer any decision, at least until he had a better feel for how things were being handled. If it was not resolved quickly, he would start looking in other directions for help. One thing that seemed clear to him was the fact that the longer Alicia remained in the hands of kidnappers, the less her chances for a safe return would be.

The officers stopped outside an office with dirty venetian blinds drawn tight on the inside and knocked on the door. McDermott turned to Aaron. "Chief wanted to speak with you when we got here, Mr. Goldman."

"Is David Boyle still Chief of Police?"

"Yes, sir. You know him?"

"We've met several times at city functions. I think he'll remember me."

"Of course I remember you, Mr. Goldman." The door was open and the large black man stood with a business-like countenance and his hand extended toward Aaron.

"I'm very sorry about your wife. You can rest assured that everything, and I mean everything, is being done that we can to find her. I know it sometimes looks a little disorganized around here, but don't let that bother you. We know what we're doing and you've got a couple of our best detectives here on it. You've been introduced?"

McDermott responded, "We met him at his office, Chief. He followed us down here. He's going to give us background material and hopefully some leads. You want to sit in with us?"

"I'll probably join you in a while. I'll tell you what, though. Would you and Clarence let me speak with Mr. Goldman alone for a moment? I'll bring him down to the briefing room in a minute."

The officers left and Chief Boyle shut the door behind them. "I know this is not easy for you, Mr. Goldman. There will undoubtedly be some questions asked that you might find offensive and I want you to understand that they would be asked of anyone in this circumstance. We can't afford to leave any possible motive or lead unchecked and we don't have a lot of time to be as civil as we would like."

"Don't worry about insulting me, Chief Boyle. I'll help any way I can to find my wife. I know where you're coming from and I understand. I'll answer any question I can."

"Good, I'm glad you do. A lot of times when people are, well, so prominent in the community as you are, they resent being questioned thoroughly. They see it as an invasion of their affairs you might say."

"That won't be a problem with me."

"Good, that's good."

"Well, let's walk down to the briefing room, shall we? By the way, I spoke to a friend of mine who is also a businessman in the area and he indicated that your company has recently gone public and that there were, as could be expected, a few disagreements over the direction the company was headed. Anyone particularly unpleasant about it?"

"Certainly not enough to abduct my wife. I can't think of anyone I know that would be even remotely capable of this. My

God! They even killed Morris, our driver. He had two kids. Whoever did this has to be pretty damned sick."

"I agree, Mr. Goldman. But unfortunately, there is no shortage of sick people these days. And, from personal experiences, I can tell you that you can't rule anybody out. So try and think of anyone you've had disputes with over the last few months. No matter how small."

"You think that this might be out of revenge and not just for money?"

"Like I said, I don't rule out anything. I'll be leaving you in here with the detectives but I'll probably join you in little while. By the way, you should be prepared to be hounded by the media the moment you leave here."

"The media? How are they involved?"

"Are you kidding? Prominent socialite, wife of a community leader is kidnapped, her chauffeur killed; they're in a feeding frenzy."

"How do they know about this already?"

"Who knows? Scanners, informants, department leaks. Can't keep secrets anymore. They seem to know what happens here about as fast as we do. Just don't discuss any details with them. Being even a day ahead of them can be tough."

"I'll just stay away from them."

Chief Boyle directed Aaron to an office across the hall as he continued. "You won't find that as easy as you might think. Well, I've got to go face the cameras. I'll leave Mr. Goldman here with you now. See you shortly."

The two detectives, Brown and McDermott, were seated in the small room at the corner of a long table. There were files thrown about on top and at the far end sat a young, attractive woman.

With her stylish, dirty blonde hair and youthful appearance, she seemed out of place in the room and especially at the moment.

Bob McDermott spoke. "Mr. Goldman, this is Freda Payne. She's a criminal psychologist and an expert in hostage and kidnapping situations. She works for the feds and works with us in many times in cases of this sort."

The young woman stood up and firmly shook Aaron's hand. "Call me Freda."

"Thank you for coming."

"It's my job, Mr. Goldman. I want to assure that we'll find out what happened to your wife. Right now, time is the enemy, so, what do you say we all sit down and go over this from the beginning?"

It was apparent that the officers deferred to the expertise of Freda Payne. She turned on a digital recorder, set it on the table and then grabbed a legal pad from her briefcase on the floor beside her. "Do you wish to have an attorney present, Mr. Goldman?"

"Good Lord, I'm not a suspect, am I?"

"No, sir. Some people just feel more comfortable with their lawyer present. Your Miranda rights certainly apply here and it's our duty to inform you that you have a right to an attorney; if you cannot afford one, one will be appointed to represent you; and whether you choose to use the services of an attorney or not, anything you say can and may be used against you. Now, with that said, if you don't think you need one, we'll get started."

"I'm fine. I'll answer anything for you that I can."

"That's great. I don't mean to upset you."

Aaron did not hesitate in his response. "There is nothing I wouldn't do to get my wife back. I love her and I want to be of any help that I can. Understand?"

Freda Payne responded matter-of-factly to his statement as if she had heard every possible reply that could have been made many times before. "I usually start with a series of standard questions that help us determine the parameters of a case and hopefully a suspect. Now, Mr. Goldman, try to relax and answer each question with as much detail as you can. If you don't remember something, just say that. Don't guess unless we ask you to. We are interested primarily in known facts, not opinions. When did you last see Mrs. Goldman?"

"Just this morning. We were going to go out tonight. I..."

"Don't get ahead of my questions please, Mr. Goldman."

"Okay. I'm sorry."

Though very professional, Freda Payne's manner could easily be mistaken for rude. She demanded complete quiet, full attention from everyone in the room, and no distractions. She steered the responses from Aaron in a specific direction and accepted only the most specific of replies. "What time was that this morning?"

"Probably seven, maybe seven fifteen."

Freda began taking extensive notes as she questioned Goldman. "Was it pleasant? Were you fighting?"

"We almost never fight. We're the best of friends."

"I'm sure. Remember, don't be offended. These are questions I would ask anyone."

"I'm fine. Go ahead."

"Mr. Goldman, how long were you together this morning?"

"Thirty, maybe forty minutes."

"Was there any sexual intimacy, either this morning or last night?"

"No. How is that relevant?"

"Sometimes under these circumstances women are raped. Any semen detected would need to be traced. We would need to know who she had been with, if anyone. It's my policy to cover all these issues now, up front, while they're fresh in your memory. This is all very standard. I actually have a preset list of questions that I work from until a specific direction develops in each case."

"I'm sorry. The question just caught me off guard. I won't do that again."

"No problem. Now, let's get back to the questions. Do you remember what your wife was wearing?"

"Just undergarments. She hadn't dressed by the time I left. Since she was going to the auction, I'm sure she would have dressed up. Probably a designer suit."

"The auction at Furman's. Where the car was found?"

"Yes, Furman's Estate Sales, I believe it's called."

"Were there any phone calls for her or you this morning or even late last night, especially someone you didn't know?"

"No. None that I remember. Wait, her sister called while she was in the shower. I took the call and Delores, that's her name, said she would call back later. I don't think she did though. That's the only one I remember. And… Wait. She's been getting a number of hang-ups."

"Hang-ups?"

"You know, a guy calls her, never speaks and after a while, just hangs up. It was beginning to unnerve her the last several times. I was going to get the phone company to try and trace them, put a stop to it."

"You said, a guy made the calls. How do you know that if the caller never speaks?"

"Well, I guess I don't really; I just assumed it must be. I've never heard of a female obscene caller calling another woman."

"You never received the calls?"

"I think I might have had a couple of quick hang-ups, but I hadn't drawn any connection to them yet. I guess it could have been the same person though."

"Okay, I want to go into these calls a little more, but I'll continue with our first series of questions and we'll come back to it."

"Fine."

"Have you or your wife been having an affair that you are aware of? I know you said you got along well, but I have to ask. No one else will know."

"Absolutely not. We love each other. Our relationship has never been better."

"Is there anyone you can think of who might want to cause you or your wife harm, either physically or financially? Do you have enemies?"

"Like anybody in business, I've had a few run-ins but none that were earth-shattering."

"I want a list of anyone you can remember having more than a friendly disagreement with in the past two years. Can you bring that to me in the morning?"

"Of course. It won't be very long. I try to keep good working relationships with people."

"How long had the driver worked for you?"

"He's been with us about four years. Alicia hates to drive, especially downtown. She's a little too high-strung to deal with all the traffic."

"Who would have known Alicia was going to the auction this morning?"

"I... I just don't know. There's a group of regulars that attend those things. They all know each other and what type of things they're interested in. There's sort of a friendly competition among them."

"Competition?"

"Sure, to see who can outbid the other without getting stung too bad on any one item. I guess you could look at it as a type of one-upmanship. You understand?"

"I think so. Sounds a lot like a competition of who's got the most money that won't be missed. Do you know if your wife has her fingerprints on file anywhere, or dental records?"

"You're making me nervous. It sounds like you think she's already dead."

"I have to ask these questions. Can we continue?"

"Go ahead. I can't seem to stop interrupting you."

"Fingerprints? Dental records?"

"Dental records I know would be at our dentist, Bob Emory in Mechanicsville. Fingerprints. I don't think she ever had a reason to have them taken."

"Neither of you has ever been arrested?"

"In college, many years ago. We were at a political demonstration with a bunch of students in Charlottesville. We all got hauled in together. That's right! They did fingerprint us. If they keep records that long, they might still have them."

"Clarence, will you check that out?"

"Done."

"Who would have knowledge of your financial condition?"

"I'm sure a lot of people think we're worth more than we are. Over the years, thousands of people have worked at our company. Most are blue collar workers and they would all consider us very wealthy, by comparison. It's a lot of people."

"And how is your financial condition right now? If you had to raise a million dollars ransom overnight, could you?"

"Yes. I would probably have to cash in a number of securities or at least borrow against them, but yes, I routinely keep a five million dollar line of credit to run the business."

"Very good. You may have to do that soon. You know Bob, Clarence... I'm thinking we better get Mr. Goldman back to his house pretty quick. It's been over five hours since the car was found. Any demands could be coming pretty soon. Get some people from Technical to set up the monitor and we'll continue this at his home. That work for you, Mr. Goldman?"

"If that's what you think is best. You're the expert."

"We better go then."

4

Aaron Goldman followed the officers through downtown Richmond, back into the exclusive Salisbury suburb where the Goldman's home was located. It appeared they were being followed by several cars through town. As he had been warned earlier, they were reporters trying to get a jump on the competition. As they made the final turn onto his oak-lined street, they were all shocked at the scene before them. The normally quiet lane was brightly lit with halogen flood lights. The tops of satellite dishes mounted on the roofs of vans and network trailers stood out above the neighbors' cars and dense shrubbery. Freda Payne directed McDermott, "Bob, better get some folks from the Sheriff's department out here. I imagine this will only be getting worse if this thing continues."

Aaron wondered if the neighbors all knew about Alicia's abduction already. The officers double parked in the street and directed the news crews to leave the driveway open for them and Goldman.

Freda didn't like the media. She felt they hampered her work and served to the benefit of criminals a lot of the time. "They've got a right to be here, granted, but they better stay the hell out of our way! And listen, I don't want any of our people or anyone involved in the investigation saying a word to them that hasn't been cleared by my office first. Got that?"

"Don't worry" Detective Brown responded. "I don't like 'em any more than you. Mr. Goldman is already worried sick about his wife and now he's got all this shit in his front yard. They're like a pack of damned vultures fighting over road kill."

Aaron pulled into the drive behind them. With no other police presence, the mob of reporters and news hounds descended on his car. He kept the doors locked and made no effort to get out. He waited for the detectives to escort him. As they opened his car door, over a dozen microphones were shoved his way and he was literally blinded by the lights from the camera crews.

"Mr. Goldman, Mr. Goldman. Any word yet from the kidnappers?" "Have any demands been made?" "When did you last see her?" "Have they found a body yet?"

Aaron had seen this kind of outlandish behavior on television but actually being the focus of such a mob was beyond imagination. He answered no questions and followed the officers into his house. He could still hear questions being yelled out as the door shut behind them. "When will we get a statement?" "Detective Payne. Will you address the media tonight?"

Aaron was glad to hear the heavy thud of his door closing behind them. Still, the glare from the floodlights filled his living room. Aaron walked around the house shutting the blinds and then returned to the waiting officers. "Sorry, I guess they got the best of me a little out there."

McDermott, disgusted at what was going on replied, "If we had known this much of a media circus was waiting, we would have gotten some people out here sooner and moved them away from the house. We'll get it straightened out in short order. To some extent we have to accommodate them, but this is ridiculous. Just cool off for a while."

Freda interrupted, "Do you have an answering machine?"

"That's right! I need to check it."

"I'll go with you. And listen, if the phone rings, don't answer yet. We want to get the line monitored, tracers in place, and recorders going. Just leave the machine on. Any calls on it?"

"It's packed. The counter shows fifteen calls."

Aaron reached to play the messages, but Freda Payne grabbed his hand firmly. "No, don't touch it. Seriously, it's important to wait just a little bit. There's a kid coming over with our tech staff that is pretty much of a wizard on this type of thing. I don't want to do anything until he looks at the setup. They can do some pretty amazing things with their computer gizmos and we don't want to lose anything that they could have used. Got a coffee machine here?"

"Uh, yeah. In the kitchen. Next door down the hall. Just tell your people to help themselves to whatever they need. I'm just not myself yet. I think I'll just take off my coat and tie and sit down for a moment. I don't recall feeling this tired in quite a while."

"It's to be expected, Aaron. Emotionally distressing situations like this can deplete you pretty damned quick. Just sit back and shut your eyes for a little bit. When our crew gets here, and we're set up, I'll come and get you."

"Thanks."

Aaron had sat back for what seemed like only seconds when the technical crew arrived. Reporters and camera crews documented their every step as they made their way into the home. There were two older men and a young man who didn't look to be over nineteen. Aaron could only assume that this must be the whiz kid Freda Payne had mentioned. He watched as they opened steel road cases and removed numerous pieces of electronic equipment and began to position them around the room. A rather large unit that looked like a recording device of some sort was set up next to the phone. Freda Payne came over to the young man.

"Thurman, this is Aaron Goldman. He's the husband of the woman who was abducted. Before you punch any holes in his walls or anything dramatic, please ask him."

"Nice to meet you, sir. I'm Thurman Roe."

Aaron, still feeling very drained, stood and shook his hand. "Call me Aaron. Just do whatever you need to. If you have to punch holes in the walls, go ahead and do it. I don't care about anything like that; it can all be fixed. Just help me find my wife."

"We'll do our best, sir. This the answering machine, Freda?"

"That's it. There's a number of calls on it but Aaron said he cleared it yesterday, so there may be something on it that you can use. And another thing, Thurman. They have been getting a 'heavy breather' for the last couple of weeks. Can you trace a hang-up from one of those?"

"Well, let me study it for a few minutes. It's a pretty high end, digital machine. It has a 'return last call' feature, so I know we can find at least that number."

Thurman produced a small, jeweler's screwdriver and began to remove the cover from the answering machine. Aaron walked over to Freda. "He's awful young. Are you sure he's…"

"The best. I've worked with computer types for years and he's as good as they get. Just watch him, you'll be impressed."

Aaron sat back down on the couch and took Freda's advice. Within a matter of minutes, another answering machine was in place and the original unit was connected to a machine that resembled an intensive care unit monitoring system with all of its lines and LED readouts. Thurman was taking in every detail and entering the results on a small laptop computer. He called to Freda, "Okay, we're set up here. I'm ready for listeners." Freda sat down beside Aaron, her ever-present legal pad in her lap.

"Aaron, he's going to play the messages on the machine. He'll start each one, you identify who the caller is if you can. We'll stop between every call and replay it if it will help."

Thurman interjected, "I've already copied the digitized information onto my unit, so if it crashes, we'll still have a good copy. Besides, my unit can do a couple of interesting things with the data. Here we go, call number one."

They listened intently to each message. The third recording seemed out of the ordinary. Aaron was the only one in the room who realized the peculiarity of the call. He asked to replay it.

"Hello, darling. It's your big sister. I was just on my way to Furman's and thought that if you were going to be there also, and I'm sure you will, why don't we have a drink and talk for a while? If you get this message before you leave, I'll just see you there. Ta ta, love."

Freda Payne was puzzled. "It's her sister, right? What's unusual about it?"

"They don't get along at all. Delores probably hasn't called the house in the past ten years. I'm certain that she wouldn't do anything to hurt Alicia, but it's just odd she called today of all days."

"It's probably just a coincidence, Aaron. If she were involved in any way, she would undoubtedly be too smart to leave a message on the machine that would stand out this much."

"I'm sure you're right."

The obvious presumption of innocence didn't keep Freda from making several notes in her pad.

"Two of the calls are from concerned family members, one from your lawyer, Burns, and the rest are from the media. That means they were made late this afternoon when the news got out. There's two hang-ups, both before her sister called which had to be fairly close to when she left for the auction. That might be our breather. I'll check it out."

"How can you tell who called?"

"If they didn't speak, I can't, but I should be able to tell where they called from. Give me a minute."

"Okay, let's go back over these other calls and try and pinpoint the times closer."

Freda played the messages again from the beginning.

"Aaron, this is Fred. Just heard about Alicia on the way home. I'll hold everything down at the office. If you need me for anything, and that's anything, buddy, just call. Diane and I will be there in a heartbeat. I'll talk to you in the morning."

Even as they listened to the messages, news organizations continued to call.

"How in the hell did they get my number? It's unlisted and unpublished!"

"Don't ask. They have so many informants today you wouldn't believe it. Tomorrow morning your high school picture could wind up in the *National Enquirer*."

An excited Thurman called out from in front of his monitor. "Now we're cooking with gas. We're gonna have numbers."

This revelation got Freda Payne excited. "How is that, Thurman?"

"Since this is a digitized unit and records the number of the last caller, it stores an internal temp file for each call. It only shows the last one on the unit's LED readout, but they're all in there. The unit holds twenty calls and it stores all of the numbers in its tiny little brain until the file is deleted when the unit is emptied to record new calls."

"You're amazing, Thurman. I told you, Aaron."

"I'm impressed. How long will it take to get the numbers out of it on the hang-ups?"

"About as long as it takes me to walk over to my laptop and download the data. Four minutes, max."

By now, the young man had quite a number of the officers around him as he pulled up the information. "Got it! Same number both times. It's a payphone."

"How can you tell?" Aaron quizzed.

This was an easy question for all the officers in the room. Clarence Brown enlightened him. "All of the payphones in the city start with the prefix 990. It lets the phone company know you're calling from one of theirs."

"Damn. Can you tell where this particular phone is located?"

"I'm sure the phone company supervisor is already on the line there with McDermott."

"I have to tell you, I am very impressed with how you are doing so far."

"Hold the pat on the back for a bit yet. Unless whoever it was is standing by that phone in an hour, we may have zero. It would surprise me if they were dumb enough to call for a ransom demand from the same phone. This doesn't strike me as amateur-hour work. I'd bet on a stolen cellular from a moving vehicle. But crazier things have happened. Clarence, after you get a location on the phone, put a surveillance team on it and tell them to stay in contact with me."

"I'm already there, Freda. But you're right; they ain't gonna be that dumb."

"Maybe not, but we can't assume that."

"You're right."

Bob McDermott was putting pieces of the puzzle together in his head and throwing them out to Freda and Clarence. "What would be the point of the 'breathing' calls? How would they play into a kidnapping?"

Freda didn't have to study for that answer. "They'd want to establish her schedule. What time she was up in the morning, if she was alone, and this morning, to tell if she had left. It might be nothing but then again, it just might be something. Tell 'em to get that phone under scrutiny, in a hurry!"

Feeling that now at least some positive steps had been made, the officers began to settle in for what would undoubtedly be a long wait, one they had all experienced before. Freda turned to Aaron. She could see that he was getting keyed up over the prospect of catching the "breather" and she knew that the odds were still quite small that they would find the caller at the payphone.

"Why don't we all just go sit down and we can finish going over the rest of these questions."

"Let's go to the kitchen. I'll make some coffee and try to get my head on straight. Have I told you anything yet that might be helpful?"

"It's still too early to tell. It's like fishing. Just because you don't get any bites doesn't mean your bait is wrong. It could be that the fish are just not hungry yet. A picture of what's going on generally develops pretty quickly. The main thing that needs to happen now is for whoever took Mrs. Goldman to try and contact you."

"Let's say that whoever took Alicia is not the 'breather.' Do you think they'll have this number too?"

"I doubt anyone would go to this much trouble without having researched Mrs. Goldman, you, and probably your entire family as well as all of your business associates. Yes, they know how to contact you. Right now, they're probably making sure that where they are is secure and maybe are even observing what's going on here."

"You mean watching us now?"

"Makes perfect sense. They'll want to know what our responses are and how significant an effort is being made to find them."

"Bastards! If you catch these perverts, I'd like to have a shot at them."

"Everybody would, Aaron. I hope you don't mind me calling you Aaron?"

"No problem. Please do."

"I feel good about this case, Aaron. We'll get your wife back."

"I wish I could be sure of that. She's a strong woman, but she was always sheltered by her father, and now I try to. I know she's probably berserk by now. I hope that no matter what else happens, we can get her back."

"I'm sure we will, Aaron."

While Freda and Aaron sat in the kitchen, Thurman ran into the room beaming with excitement. "We have our first possible break!"

Freda jumped up spilling her coffee on the table. "Someone calling with demands?"

"Negative. Just got a call from a credit card supervisor. Somebody's using her cards."

Aaron also stood up. "Did they catch him?"

"Not yet. Wait, there's more. Mrs. Goldman's cell phone had two long distance calls made on it within the hour. We're in contact with the provider and they will let us know in short order which tower the calls were made from. That should narrow down the area the suspect is in. The bank owning the ATM where the withdrawal attempt was made is pulling the video tape as we speak. We should have a look at who was trying to use her credit card within the hour."

Freda looked at Aaron, smiled and then turned back to face Thurman. "That's great work. Stay on top of this. I want to know everything that happens, instantly."

"You got it, boss lady."

Freda called all of the detectives and investigators into the kitchen. "I guess you all heard a minute ago that we've got our first lead. The kidnapper has tried to use Mrs. Goldman's credit card and has made two long distance calls on her cell phone. The bank that owns the ATM is checking user video to get us a photo and the phone company is getting us the tower information. We also need to find out who was on the other end of those two phone calls and track them down. Get them to tell us just who they were talking to and what the call was about. And of course we want background checks on these individuals. I want to know everything about them from who they went to the senior prom with to where their dogs got their rabies shots."

She turned to Detectives Brown and McDermott. "Clarence, you can handle the phone company. Bob, you get the video. Have Thurman help you pull the best still shot of our suspect from it. Have it enhanced as much as possible, then make copies and hit the streets near the tower that handled the cell calls."

"Yes, ma'am."

The two officers left the room immediately. It was not difficult to see the wheels turning in Freda's head. Aaron laid his hand on her arm to get her attention. "How significant is this?"

"Could be the entire case. Let's just hope she's still alive. The suspect didn't get cash which means he doesn't know her PIN. That could go either way. She may have been able to give him one that didn't work or convince him she didn't know it... Or, she might not be able to tell anyone anything. We'll just have to find him and use some pressure to get him to tell us where she is."

"God, I hope she's alright."

"We all do, Aaron."

Minutes seemed like hours as the evening turned to night. Freda was still up talking with the officers and Aaron was sitting at the kitchen table staring out a window that offered a view of nothing as it was pitch black outside. Around 2 a.m., Freda shook Aaron's shoulders from behind. "Aaron, you awake?"

"Yes, I'm sorry. I must have dozed off. Didn't mean to."

"I know you must be exhausted. I just wanted to let you know. We have a location for where the phone was used and names of who received the calls. Officers are on their way in Detroit and Washington, D.C. to grab these individuals and find out what they know. Also, and more significantly, we have a pretty decent photo of the person who tried to use the credit card at the ATM. He's white, maybe thirty and pretty drugged-out looking. We have patrol officers working the streets near convenience and liquor stores in the area of the cell tower in the hope that someone might recognize him. We should be hearing something before long."

Though thoroughly spent, Aaron fought sleep. Around dawn Bob McDermott and Freda woke him. "Aaron, sorry to wake you again. We have some developments now in the case."

"What's that mean?"

"The suspect is a smalltime drug dealer and addict. Everyone our officers showed his picture to recognized him. They tracked him down to a sleazy motel and they're getting ready to go in after him right now. I knew you'd want to know."

"I do. God, I hope this ends the nightmare."

The Edgewater Motel was basically a dump on the outskirts of Richmond. The entire area was infested with drug dealers, addicts, and every sort of lowlife individual the city had to offer. Other than an occasional squad car driving the pot-holed streets responding to a robbery or an overdose victim's body in a gutter, the police generally just stayed away. Another addict's body meant there was just one less problem to deal with.

This case had far greater impact than just the area the suspect lived in. This kidnapping had shaken the core of the highly connected elite in the area. The politicians and authorities would not and could not rest until the case was solved. A large group of uniformed officers and a S.W.A.T team moved in on the motel as sunrise had barely started to illuminate the tops of the trees on the street. The highly trained squad moved into position. Two officers with a battering device stood at the ready on the front porch. A few curious residents stood across the street watching the events unfold with moderate interest. This was not the first drug bust they'd seen.

At the precise choreographed moment, the ram removed the flimsy veneer door from its frame, shattering it, and black-suited officers stormed into the dark motel room. Other than officers yelling for the suspect to put his hands behind his head and to freeze, nothing could be heard. There were no shots and no screams. In less than two minutes the suspect, wearing only a dirty jogging suit bottom and tee shirt, his hands behind his back in cuffs, was led to a waiting squad car. Other officers were pulling yellow crime scene tape across the door to the motel room as the suspect was driven downtown.

Aaron waited anxiously at his home until Freda showed back up late that afternoon. "Well, we have some answers. Some good, some not so good."

"What did you find out? Did he still have her?"

"No. He never had her. He's a smalltime creep. He was at the back of the parking lot trying to steal a stereo out of a car when he heard someone yelling for help. He went towards where he'd heard the sound and found Alicia's driver lying on the ground dying. Apparently, her pocketbook with her wallet, credit cards, and cell phone was just lying on the ground near the limousine. He grabbed the purse and ran. He said he saw a car pulling off down the street. He said he couldn't tell what model it was other than it was a large, nondescript, grey sedan. Not much help there."

"You believe him."

"Yes. He's a three-time loser. After years of drug abuse, he has the IQ of a shovel. He couldn't have engineered this on his best day. After he discovered that he couldn't get any money from the ATM without Alicia's number, he sold the credit cards to a gang member he knew downtown for fifty bucks."

"And the phone calls?"

"One was to his mother and the other one was another addict he used to hang with. We spoke with both of them and there just wasn't anything there. So, after striking out with the cards he took the fifty bucks and immediately got juiced up on dope and collapsed in the hotel room where we found him. We're tracking down the gang member who bought the cards but I doubt any of this is going to give us the leads we need to find Alicia. I'm afraid the one thing we learned from this is not good news."

"What's that?"

"Whoever took her wasn't interested in robbing her. Her pocketbook was left on the ground and they never even checked it for credit cards or cash. It was intact when our druggy found it. So, she wasn't taken by a petty thief or a gang of some sort. I'm sorry. But we are just getting started here. Don't give up. We've got some calls out for additional help and we hope to have some forensic experts here in the next day or so. They'll examine things and come up with leads we can't even fathom. You go get some sleep now. We'll wake you if anything happens. You can't keep going with no rest."

* * *

A quick resolution, good or bad, did not occur. After two full days of no sleep and waiting for a call from the abductors, the original optimism was giving way to doubts of all sorts. By now, the Goldman home was full of plainclothes and uniformed officers. Some were maintaining crowd control outside for what was becoming a full-blown media circus. Others were technical experts waiting for the call that had not come. And still others tried to piece together what few clues they could and decide on a course of action. Chief Boyle was now present as well as two hostage experts from the State Bureau of Investigation. Aaron Goldman was exhausted mentally and physically and a growing concern for the fate of Alicia was taking its toll on his state of mind. Chief Boyle addressed the others.

"I think we're all in agreement that this kidnapping is at a critical stage. The abductors may have gotten cold feet when they realized that they had underestimated the amount of attention that this would draw. Perhaps they are revising their contact plans and will look for a third party such as someone in the media to approach. They would, of course, absolutely love that turn of events. If the first scenario is correct, then as you all know, that would be the worst blow to our chances of getting Mrs. Goldman returned safely.

"Finally, some of you have already indicated you are inclined to feel this may not be a kidnapping at all, but a homicide. That possibility does exist, as much as we would all hate to find out that is the case. No matter which of these is correct, one thing is certain, we can't wait any longer for the kidnappers to contact us. Time is our enemy. So, I have spoken with Mrs. Anne Coltrain who owns a local television station with a major network affiliate and told her we would like to hold a press conference two hours from now.

"Mr. Goldman would like to appeal to the kidnappers to spare his wife and assure them that he will meet any conditions necessary to have her returned. At that point, if they respond and make demands, we will have to back off in an attempt to save her life. If and when she is returned, we'll re-enter with a maximum effort and try to apprehend them after that point. Freda, how about going over Mr. Goldman's outline and making sure that the right things are said. The rest of you, stand by and keep your minds running. We'll win this thing yet."

* * *

Once again, the bright lights forced Aaron Goldman's eyes to become small black pinpoints as he addressed the large crowd of reporters and media types that had been increasing in number for the past several days. He was used to addressing public groups and the media but he felt the pressure this time like no other time before. His throat was dry and the words didn't flow as they normally would.

"Good evening. My name is Aaron Goldman. I would like to thank everyone for their support who has been here during this time. I would like to address the person or individuals who took my wife two days ago. We are waiting to hear from you. I am prepared to do whatever it takes to get my wife back."

Goldman, for the first time, fought back tears as he pleaded for his wife's safe return. "I love my wife very much and ask you to put yourself in my place. There is no amount of money or anything that I have that I would not give to get her back. The police have agreed to not interfere with any ransom procedures that you require. Please call... Please. Again, thank you all for being here."

The lights and cameras followed him as he returned to the house from the hastily set up platform on his front porch. Freda Payne walked beside him.

"Let's hope they were listening, Freda."

"Unless they're in a cave, they'll hear it. The news media will play it repeatedly for at least a couple of days. Maybe we'll get a call soon."

"God, I hope so. I'm beginning to wear down."

"Hang in there, Aaron. Don't give up."

"That... I will never do."

                                        * * *

Planter's Run was one of the premier "watering holes" of the upper-crust set in Richmond. It had been said, and often repeated, that more money changed hands there at lunchtime than on the floor of the New York Stock Exchange in a week. Financial circles knew well the amount of old, "heavy money" that circulated in Richmond, just one of the country's top banking and insurance centers. This day was no exception. The many dark cubicles literally bristled with the air of affluence that overwhelmed the ostentatious interior of the restaurant. As with most places of its type, Planter's Run had its VIP section to flatter those who thought their position in the business community deserved a little extra attention. And then, of course, it had its very special areas where those who really did control the wealth and power of the city conducted their business with no interruption. Even the waiters who attended to these patrons had developed a feel for when a conversation had reached the proper point for them to serve the meal or drinks. Delores Thompson, Alicia's older, and much more socially in tune, sister sat at one such table with her stockbroker, Angus McVeigh. Angus had a well-earned reputation as the one man in town that knew, in advance, what business transactions of any magnitude were about to take place. In fact, he was the instrument that made most of them fly.

"Nobody is to know anything about this until after I have secured enough stock to take over the board. That's clear, isn't it?"

"Delores, darling. You've known me how many years now? You have to ask that?"

"This time is different, Angus. A foul-up here would not only be extremely embarrassing; it could cost me, and consequently you, a great deal of money."

"You're talking about more than a great deal of money. Certainly, you have some securities stored away that even I don't know about. Your rivalry with your sister must be pretty intense to undertake such a venture. Your wealth is very stable and diversified now. You realize that you'd be putting all of your eggs in one basket by trying to pull a raid on Virginia Industrial's common shares?"

"Why Angus, I'm ashamed of you for thinking that. I love my sister. This is just business. Family's very important to me. It's just that money... Well, that's real important too. Not to mention, I'm practically having an orgasm just thinking about the moment when I send her worthless husband packing. That will be my first act as the new Chairman of VI."

"A lot of the business community is going to think that you picked a very poor moment to do this, Delores, what with the kidnapping and all."

"The little shit needs to raise a great deal of money now, so I'm told. He's preparing to divest himself of a significant amount of stock to have the funds that will undoubtedly be asked for to buy Alicia's freedom. I mean, we all want my darling sister back, safe and sound. So, Angus, you know what I want. My banker will call your office this afternoon and extend to you a line of credit to begin buying the stock. Try and buy the large lots first before the price reflects the offer to buy. I don't want to pay a premium for every share I buy."

"You don't have to explain that to me, darling. You know that's what I do. Better than anyone, I might add."

"Wonderful, Angus. Well, I have to run. Remember, confidentiality. Not even a hint to anyone. No matter whose devotion you think this might buy."

"I understand completely, Delores. Have a good day."

As the tall, slender, haughty woman paraded past numerous patrons who acknowledged her presence, the illustrious broker murmured to himself, "What a bitch!" The expression on his face then changed to the plastic smile and more constant expression of a self-confident financier. "Waiter, you have something for me to sign?"

5

The first thing Alicia noticed was the overpowering dryness in her throat. Her lips were stuck together and there was a bitter taste in her mouth. She was so disoriented that it took several minutes to realize that she had been out. Not asleep, but unconscious. She was lying on a bed in a dark room. Only a small ray of illumination coming from under the door to the small cubicle of a room offered any relief to the utter blackness of her surroundings. She sat up on the edge of the bed and slowly attempted, with her head still swimming, to get her bearings.

"Is anyone there? Hello…"

No answer. She tried to stand and walk to the door but fell back onto the bed. She was far weaker than she first realized. She thought to herself, *"Damn, must have passed out. I'm in a hospital or clinic."*

She detected the sound of footsteps on linoleum beyond the door and headed in her direction.

"Hello, is anybody there?"

There was a fumbling sound with keys and then the clicking of the door knob turning until it sprung open the latch. Seconds later, a fluorescent light blinked on overhead. As she focused on it, the hazy blur quickly became a clear fixture. She looked toward the door.

"Mrs. Goldman, how do you feel?"

"A little disoriented and lightheaded. Where am I? Richmond Medical Center? Did I pass out or take a fall?"

"I'm afraid not. You're a very long way from Richmond, Virginia."

"What do you mean? I haven't gone anywhere? Where are we?"

"First, let me introduce myself. My name is Kale but everyone calls me Doctor K. You're in my private diagnostic clinic. And please accept my apology for not being here when you woke up. I had intended to be present but got involved in another matter. I hope these strange new surroundings didn't frighten you. Now, as I was saying, you are under my care here in the clinic."

"What for? Did I faint or have a stroke or something?"

"Nothing quite so dramatic, Alicia. May I call you Alicia?"

"Of course. Where are we?"

Alicia tried to stand again. And again, her knees fell away from under her. Doctor K caught her and gently set her back on the bed. "Dear, I'm afraid you're not up to getting around just yet. You should lie back down for a little longer and then we'll talk about why you're here."

In his left hand, all ready for action, Doctor K held a small syringe which he raised to her arm. "I'm going to have to give you a shot, dear, to prevent infection. It will make you feel better, much better." He quickly injected her before she could speak.

"I... I... Oh... I'm so dizzy... And sleepy..."

"I know, dear. Just lie back and sleep a while."

After what seemed to her the deepest and most comfortable of sleeps, Alicia awoke once more. This time, the dryness in her mouth was gone but she felt very hungry with a slight burning in her stomach. She immediately felt a craving for something sweet.

As her head cleared, she again realized that she was not at home. She was in the same small, dark room. This time, there was a small night lamp on the table beside her, giving a dim glow to the surroundings. She studied them. The room was tiny with the single bed she was sitting on, a naugahyde chair that looked as if it was from a waiting room of some sort and a short, folding director's chair. There were a few old copies of Reader's Digest on the table and other than a pitcher of water and a single plastic cup, that was the complete inventory of the barren room.

The footsteps recurred as if on cue to her waking, and in moments the doorknob was turning again. There, entering the room and locking the door behind him was the same, strange little man she had met before.

"Doctor Maye?"

"Close, Alicia. Doctor K, as in O-K. How are you feeling today?"

"Today? How long was I out?"

"Well, you've not been totally out. You've been in and out for three days or so."

"Good Lord. What's wrong with me? What am I doing here? What about Aaron, my husband? Does he know where I am? Where am I?"

"Questions, questions, and more questions. My goodness but you are a curious sort. I'll answer some of them for you. No, I haven't really had the opportunity to contact anyone and as far as where you are... As I told you earlier, you're in my private clinic, which is not in Virginia."

"What the hell are you talking about? Not in Virginia? Just where is 'not in Virginia'? Uh... Oh... I..."

Alicia started to get very lightheaded again. In a flash, Doctor K sat her back down on the bed and, again, his ever-present hypodermic found its way to her arm. She was overcome by a serene feeling of warmth and security and leaned back in the bed. "I... Um... Thanks, Doc... K... Thanks... I..."

As she lay in an induced stupor on the bed, Doctor K smiled and turned to leave. "Don't thank me. Thank your newfound friend that's dancing in your veins."

* * *

Aaron Goldman had taken every course of action he could think of. The police had pursued the smallest of leads and nothing of substance had materialized. It was as if Alicia had just evaporated. Though no one said it to him outright, it was apparent to everyone involved in the investigation that the focus had changed from that of a kidnapping to a homicide. It had been a month since she had been abducted and there had been no ransom demands or contact of any kind by kidnappers. Aaron had racked his brain trying to come up with a suspect who might want to hurt him this much. He kept wondering how anyone could do something this detestable.

Freda Payne had been a singular positive force through all of the trauma. She had called earlier in the morning asking could she bring someone over to meet him at his office after work. Open to any suggestions at this point, especially someone he trusted as much as he did Freda, he immediately agreed. Besides, his contributions at the office had dwindled steadily since Alicia's disappearance. He was more than preoccupied and everyone around him was concerned over his state of mind. It was becoming a matter of concern for those closest to him. Something good needed to occur, and soon.

It was 7 p.m. and Freda was due at any moment. It was storming frantically with torrents of rain beating down and explosive eruptions of thunder every few minutes. Aaron figured they would be late due to the weather. He sat in the empty lobby and stared down the drive into the night waiting for a sign of their headlights. Shortly they appeared and he moved to the door, holding it open to help them escape the rain as quickly as possible. They entered, but were soaked. "Good evening, Aaron. What a mess out there!"

"Yeah, I kind of enjoy watching it but driving in it is another thing."

"Aaron, this is Aubrey Pryor. He's the gentleman I told you about. Your company attorney, Fred Burns knew of him and suggested that we enlist his help. I couldn't agree more."

Pryor was a very nondescript man. In his fifties, balding and wearing Ben Franklin type glasses, his wet, disheveled suit made him look all the more like a low rung clerk at a convenience store.

"Mr. Pryor, I'm Aaron Goldman."

"Oh, yes, yes, sir, nice to meet you. I'm Aubrey, Aubrey Pryor, like she said. Gosh, I'm soaked." He noticed the wet area on the pale blue carpet in the lobby. "I'm sorry. We're messing up your rug here."

"It's fine. Would you like a cup of coffee to warm you up?"

"Sounds wonderful to me, Aaron. How about you Aubrey?"

"Yes, ma'am. That would be fine."

They followed Goldman into the employees' lounge. He poured them both a cup and they all seated themselves at a small table. After removing their drenched coats and taking a few sips of coffee, Freda explained why she had brought the rather unimpressive-looking Mr. Pryor with her, "Mr. Pryor is a rather unique individual, Aaron."

"How's that?"

"He is one of the best private investigators in the country. He combines the knowledge and skills gained from over twenty years in the FBI's Forensic Lab in D.C. with the insights he developed over the past eight years in business for himself. He works on rather difficult cases, such as yours. He's got a very impressive track record for solving cases when the mainstream authorities had thrown in the towel. I can't help but think that he would be a valuable asset in this case. I furnished him with the folder on Mrs. Goldman and we talked this afternoon about how things stand right now."

"Do you think you could help here, Mr. Pryor?"

"Well, I'm certainly intrigued. First though, I'll have to put the case and all of its myriad ramifications together in my mind. I work kind of like a strainer. I pour all of the pieces, fact and fiction, together and, in theory, only relative facts wind up getting through the sieve. I let it all settle for a few days and then I get an impression of the situation, based on the facts and my own intuition. I have to admit, this is a rather bizarre case. It runs contrary to the usual kidnapping or abduction-murder scenario. A lot of unanswered questions in my mind. One thing is jumping out at me in spades though."

"What's that?"

"Professional… You are dealing with an individual, or individuals, that know exactly what they're doing. That of course affects the motive, even our chances of solving this puzzle. It also makes it very interesting to me. It's the sort of thing I look for when I consider taking on an assignment."

Freda interjected, "Mr. Pryor's services are in great demand."

The unusual little man produced a toothpick from somewhere in his trousers and picked at his teeth, occasionally sucking wind between the newly cleaned channels as he spoke. This peculiar habit was disgusting to watch, but Aaron felt he could put up with just about anything that might resolve the recent events in his life.

"In reality, Mr. Goldman, I only take about one out of a hundred requests for my services. I am retired, you know. This is something I do out of a lifelong fascination with the intricacies of the criminal mind. I feel I have a good understanding of the thought processes they use, in most cases. My instincts, as 'most any seasoned investigator will probably tell you, are my best tool.'"

"God knows, I've tried everything anyone has suggested. Would you consider taking this on?"

"That's why I'm here, Mr. Goldman. I assume you understand that this is not an inexpensive undertaking. You would have to cover all of my expenses, any resources that I might need to access, and my fee which is five hundred dollars a day."

"I don't care what it costs. I want my wife back and I'm afraid that we're running out of time."

"Good. Consider me part of your team. As she said, Detective Payne has already given me a copy of the case file. I am building a list in my mind of things I would like for you to get for me and, of course, I need for you to set aside some time for me tomorrow so that I can run any questions that I might have past you."

"That's fine with me. Just tell me where and when you want to meet. I'll do it right now if you want."

"Detective Payne will set it up tomorrow. Tonight, could you go through any photo albums you might have and bring all the pictures you can find of Mrs. Goldman that have been taken in, say, the past five years?"

"Absolutely! And, Mr. Pryor…"

"Yes?"

"What do you think the chances of finding Alicia alive could be after this long?"

"I'll tell you tomorrow after I've gotten more of the facts pieced together. One thing though I can assure you."

"What's that?"

"Whether we are fortunate enough to find your wife alive or otherwise, Mr. Goldman, I will find out what happened to her. On that you can be certain."

"That's reassuring, Mr. Pryor. I've been waiting quite some time to hear somebody say that."

The exceedingly strange Mr. Pryor arose and went back out into the stormy evening. Aaron looked over at Freda. "You have great confidence in this gentleman, don't you?"

"He's not as tame as he looks. He's solved dozens of very high profile cases."

"Abductions?"

"Yes. One in particular comes to mind. Do you remember the case in Florida of the guy who owned a bunch of car dealerships and his daughter was kidnapped? She was gone for over a month. The Miami cops and all their best investigators turned up nothing. The father hired Aaron Pryor and he found her in just under two weeks. Turns out the girl had been abducted and tortured beyond belief. Aubrey tracked down this demented serial killer through tire tracks and the DNA on a cigarette butt. He used all of the suspect's past acquaintances and family members to develop a profile and where to look. He analyzed all the available information and solved the case."

"And the girl?"

"Unfortunately, she was dead by the time they found her. The killer got his too. Took a .45 caliber slug between the eyes when he tried to pull a weapon on our shy looking Mr. Pryor. Believe me, he's up to the task or I wouldn't have brought him in on this case."

Alive with a new burst of enthusiasm, Aaron sat down in the darkened lobby and thought back over the past thirty days. He stared silently out of the large lobby windows into the dark night, watching the intermittent lightning flashes illuminate the sky.

* * *

"Alicia, darling, you're awake. Very good. Goodness, you've been in dreamland for the longest time. Today is a very special day for you. It's not only your one month anniversary here in the clinic, but it is the first day of your new life."

The words reverberated in her head as if they were being screamed down through a manhole into the bowels of the city sewage system. By the time the first sentence registered through her fogged mind, the entire paragraph was over. All she could manage to do was ask, "What... What did you say? Where am I?"

The words came out in an agonizingly slow procession as if she was just learning to pronounce them for the first time as she said them. Doctor K went over and stood beside her. He picked her up and helped her move toward a stout, straight-backed chair with straps located strategically on it to render its occupant motionless. It resembled an antique electric chair minus any electrical hookups.

He eased her into it and then securely tightened the straps around her. She was like a limp, life-sized doll. She moved in whatever direction he pushed and offered no resistance to him of any fashion. To hear him speak, one could easily think him the typical Norman Rockwell stylized family doctor. Thoughtful, considerate, with a gentle touch and quiet manner, he appeared to be the most sympathetic of physicians with his patient.

"Now Alicia, I'm sure that you're not getting a lot of what I'm saying right now, so, I'm going to just let you sit here for a while and revisit with us on earth. I need to determine just how badly you require your 'medicine' at this point. I'm willing to bet you just about don't want to live without it. I think the best course of action is to leave you here to your thoughts for a couple of hours." He patted her unresponsive head as he left.

Alicia stared blankly toward the wall. A full thirty seconds after he left the room, she said quietly, "Bye…"

For the first hour, Alicia tried to focus her thoughts, to find a way out of the dark cloud that covered her mind. After sleeping almost non-stop for so long, she still felt the overwhelming need to just close her eyes and drift away to a place where dreams seemed to be calling her. This was the longest period of time that she had been left alone and without Doctor K immediately giving her a shot of the sedative he had been undoubtedly using on her. While expecting him to walk in any moment, she began to become more clearheaded and cognizant of her surroundings. She soon became aware that she desperately needed a bath. Her own body odor found its way to her senses and she wished that she could just be at home, in the large whirlpool tub that adjoined her bedroom. *How wonderful that would be. And, Aaron would be there. Aaron, where was he? Where was she?* The clearer her mind became, the more it was flooding with questions. And, there was still this intense burning in her stomach. And her hands and feet were beginning to itch unmercifully. She needed something to ease the burning before she dissolved.

As promised, Doctor K returned after several hours had passed. Alicia's eyes now had a little more life in them. The best that could be said of her appearance was that she looked terrible. Her long dark hair was matted and twisted against her head and neck. There were huge dark circles under her eyes, her cheeks pale and hollow looking. She had lost at least twenty pounds and resembled more a street person than the statuesque beauty she had been only thirty days before.

"Back among the living, are you?"

"I'm hungry. I need water."

"I'm sure you do. You've eaten practically nothing for a month. If it hadn't been for your intravenous feeding, you would be a skeleton by now I'm sure. I'll be glad to fix you a little something. I'll bet you're particularly hungry right now. How do you feel?"

"I want to go home. Why are you keeping me?"

"Science, my dear. The pursuit of knowledge. You are helping me to conduct a series of tests that I'm particularly interested in. You, beautiful Alicia, have been receiving a rather large and continual dosage of heroin for a full month. You've been almost comatose in a drugged stupor for most of that time. I'm willing to bet that you are hooked beyond redemption. You are now a full-fledged junkie."

"That's bullshit! I'm not an addict. I don't use drugs, ever!"

"Maybe not before but, trust me, you do now. It won't be long and you'll be needing a 'fix.' I can assure you of that. You've had a dope addict's wet dream for the past few weeks. Unlimited, high quality heroin, as much as you could stand. Here, take a bite of this."

He pressed a sandwich to her mouth and she took a large bite. Doctor K gave her a few sips of water to wash down each bite. After less than half of the sandwich was eaten, she was full. Her shrunken stomach needed very little to make her feel satisfied.

"You sit back and rest a little bit now. I'll be close by if you 'require' anything else. Just call me."

He had a sardonic smile on his face as he went to the laboratory bench. On the counter was the vial of white powder that he had been using to addict Alicia. He hummed while he prepared another syringe for her. That done, he cut on a small radio. It was tuned to a classical music channel and he seemed enthralled by the melody. He straightened up the room and then filled a white porcelain pan with warm water. Bringing a bar of soap and a rag with him, he went back over to Alicia and slowly began washing her. Every time he would touch her, she would flinch and grimace as if revolted by him. It was all to no avail as she was firmly secured to the chair and he seemed to enjoy her resistance.

"My, my, Alicia. You certainly are the proud one. I must tell you, dear, you don't smell the best. I have only pan-bathed you a couple of times since you've been here and you need a little freshening if we are going to be working together this afternoon. This is a little something I'm doing for myself and you'll just have to bear with me. Personal hygiene is very important. You know, first impressions being as important as they are. Starting with her feet, he moved inside and out of the white hospital gown she had been wearing since her first day in the clinic. There was no part of her body that he did not explore, not so much as to wash her, but equally as much to let her know that she was completely under his control and she might as well get used to it. It was the first hand other than her husband's to touch her genitals in many years. It made her skin crawl, but it soon became obvious that there was nothing she could do to resist.

"That's fine, I understand completely. And, the faster you get your heart pumping, the faster you're going to feel the need for your 'medicine.'"

He continued washing her.

"I am not an addict. I don't take drugs. I don't take drugs…" After a while she grew quiet.

Doctor K put the wash pan back up and walked over to her. "I'll be back in two hours and we'll talk again. You be sweet now."

Alicia stared at her surroundings. The room was now brightly lit with the overhead fluorescent lamp and for the first time in a month she was conscious enough to fully comprehend that she was being held captive and that her abductor was not a reasonable person. She was in trouble. After an hour or so racking her brain trying to decide what if anything she could do to help herself, she felt the ever expanding emptiness in her stomach and her head was beginning to throb. She was beginning to understand only too well that the hunger and need she was experiencing was not being generated by the lack of food. With each passing moment it intensified. Her pulse felt as though a runaway freight train was making its rounds inside of her. A horrible realization was staring her in the face. She needed the needle. She was addicted to the disgusting white powder that this bastard had been pumping her full of. She thought to herself, *"I'll fight it. I'll resist the need and eventually it will go away. I can do this."*

Each passing minute seemed to be longer than the preceding one. Never before had she felt such a need for anything, not even in her dreams. "Oh God. I want it so bad. I need it so bad. Doctor K! Doctor K, you bastard, come here! I need the fucking needle. Do you hear me, you asshole?"

"Now, now, dear. You don't have to talk dirty to get my attention. I was just outside the door. So, you feel you might be needing a hit, do you? I told you, sweetheart, you are now a total and hopeless drug addict, not a particularly enviable thing to be. However, I should also point out to you in no uncertain terms that you are very dependent on dear old Doctor K. I have more of the beautiful white powder than you will ever use."

"Give it to me, damn it!"

"Patience, patience. We need to wait just a little longer. I want you to realize fully what doing without this wonderful substance feels like so we won't have to go through this little procedure again."

"Please. I'll do what you want. I'll do anything. Just give me the fucking shot! DO YOU HEAR ME?"

"I do, my sweet, I certainly do. Just one more hour and you can have all you want. Just an hour. Only sixty minutes."

The sweat was pouring from her body like a garden hose was inside of her. The itching was unbearable; her head ached as though it would split; and her stomach seemed to be digesting itself. The next hour passed as if it had been a month. There was now no doubt in her mind as to the sad state of her existence. She was, as described by Doctor Kale, a drug addict of the highest magnitude. She didn't care why he did this to her. She didn't care what she looked like, smelled like, where she was, or if he was going to kill her with an overdose from the needle. He could inject it into her eyeball if he wanted. She just needed the needle as she had never needed anything so desperately in her life before. She had a new lover, a new reason to live, something so powerful that other thoughts could not enter her mind when her veins were without the chemical that owned her soul. Doctor K walked past her, smiling at her obvious state of desperation. His countenance had changed dramatically. He now appeared to be an emperor, a God who controlled her every breath. And, the delight on his face was unmistakable.

He slowly walked over to the bench and brought the hypodermic with him. He carried a latex tube in the other hand.

"It's time you learned to do this for yourself. I'm not always going to be around for you, Alicia, and you'll more than likely be doing this for the rest of your life."

He freed her hands from the straps. She kept grabbing for the needle but Doctor K forced her to tie off her forearm and find a vein. Totally oblivious to anything else in the world, she injected the heroin into herself and threw her head back in the chair. As it began to take hold, she rocked back and forth until she regressed back into her trance-like stupor and just stared at Doctor K.

"Now Alicia, let's begin stage two of our experiment. Let's start creating the new and totally different Alicia." He re-strapped her into the chair as he spoke. "And, for your new life, a new name is in order. From now on, your name is Agnes. Yes, I like that. Had an aunt named Agnes. So, that's who you'll be. And now, Agnes, let's do something about that nasty mop of hair."

He took the pan again and filled it with water. He walked over behind Alicia setting the container on the bed which was next to her chair. He then took a large pair of scissors from the lab bench and proceeded to cut off all but the smallest amount of hair from her head. The long auburn tresses fell over her shoulders and onto the floor all around her. This done, he poured a container of peroxide into the pan, mixing it in with the water and then sponged it liberally on her head. She gave no acknowledgment of the cold water on her head. She was in another world. He rinsed her hair thoroughly and then left her in the chair, drenching wet and beginning to become someone else entirely. If Aaron or, for that matter, her own mother had walked into the room, they would not have recognized her. And Doctor K had only begun to work his magic. The body was easy to change. The soul was another matter altogether.

6

Aubrey Pryor was proving to be a very unique individual. His propensity to find importance in the most obscure details was a wonder to Aaron Goldman. For the first time in weeks, he had hope. Maybe they would not be able to find Alicia alive, but he felt that they would certainly find out who took her and why. Everyone had told him that resolution and closure were critical to his own wellbeing, that not knowing was a lifelong curse. Aaron was looking forward to a status meeting with Pryor this morning. He had been studying the case for over a week and surely by now, some revelation must be at hand.

"Now Mr. Goldman, I have a few questions that I must ask you concerning some of these old photos that you gave me of your wife."

"Go ahead, and please, Aubrey, I keep telling you... Call me Aaron."

"Yes, of course, I keep forgetting. Where was I? Oh yes, this photo here. Who is this person in this picture with Mrs. Goldman? I assumed it was her father since I see him in a number of other photos as well."

"Exactly. That was just before he died back in 1986. He was very close to his children."

"And the other young woman? That is her sister. Correct?"

"Right again. How can you tell?"

"Just by the resemblance and the process of elimination."

"The sister, is she still alive?"

"Very much so."

"There is resentment between the two?"

"You're unreal, Aubrey. What made you ask that?"

"They're never in the pictures together with their father. Obvious competition for his attention. A very common scenario. How do they get along now?"

"Fight like cats and dogs. I think they probably love each other down deep, but you'd never know it to see them together."

"I'd like to meet her, if that would be possible."

"I'm sure she would be glad to help. She calls every few days to see if I've heard anything. I suspect she's also making sure that I'm getting along okay. I'll call her and arrange it."

"That would be wonderful, Aaron. Please, though, I must ask that you let me totally direct the conversation. A lot of times it might seem as though I don't have a specific purpose to a question or statement, but the majority of time that is not the case. Questioning someone is a very precise science and you will never get a first response to a question more than once. You understand, don't you?"

"Absolutely. You handle this any way you think best. I'll set it up for tomorrow evening."

"That will be just fine."

Delores Thompson met her brother-in-law and Aubrey Pryor at the door and escorted them to the parlor of her spacious brownstone townhouse. "You haven't been here in a number of years, have you, Aaron?"

"That's right, Delores. What with all the problems you and Alicia had with each other, it just never came up. You do have a lovely place though."

"That's one of the advantages of not being straight, dear boy. The male friends I have are great with interiors. Most straight men tend to just make a mess. Not that you aren't welcome, because of course, you are. Well, gentlemen, take a seat and tell me what I can do for you. I'm sure this must be about Alicia or why else would you be here?"

"It is, Delores. Let me introduce you to Aubrey Pryor. I have hired him to help find Alicia."

"Oh, a private dick, are you?"

"Yes, ma'am. I thought that you might be willing to answer a few questions for me in an attempt to get a clearer picture of Alicia in my mind. Her personal habits, friends, and such things."

"I trust that you don't suspect that I abducted my own sister for money? I am not without means, myself."

"Of course not, Miss Thompson, but I think it's pretty clear by now that this is not a ransom situation. There have been no demands made at all. In fact, whoever took her has made no contact with anyone."

"No ransom demands?" Her mind racing over this obvious flaw in her own plans, Delores shot back. "And that means?"

"Another motive altogether. Perhaps revenge, love, or mutual hatred."

"Voila! Enter Delores. Just for the record, I didn't hate Alicia. I just resent a lot of the things she does, the way we relate to one another. You know, some people are just so different that they can never be friends. I like to think of our relationship in those terms."

"Didn't…?"

"What?"

"You said you *didn't* hate her, as if you suspect she may be deceased."

"Good Lord, you're about as paranoid as they come, aren't you? I merely meant that I have not hated… See, past, up to the present. That's all. Do you have any straight-up questions for me or should I consider this a game of some sort that we are playing?"

"I have any number of questions I need help with, Miss Thompson. How was Alicia Goldman regarded by her other acquaintances as far as you know?"

"She had a few hangers-on. People in our 'station,' if you will, attract a large number of people we do not regard as friends but associating with them is mutually beneficial. Obviously, we know some better than others."

"And did she seem to get along well with most of these people?"

"As far as I know. She didn't let anyone get really close enough to her so that they could grow to dislike her."

"You don't have to answer this, but you both came from quite a wealthy family I understand."

"Yes, that's correct."

"Were you both treated the same inheritance-wise?"

"On paper, yes."

"On paper?"

"My father knew of my sexual preferences and he disapproved to say the very least. He was very parochial. Even though he divided the cash and property equally between us, he left all of the stock in Virginia Industrial to her. I got bought off, you could say. I got cash equal to the stock, but I was shut out of the family business. That way, the reputation of the real love of his life would not be smutted up by his lesbian daughter. Virginia Industrial was always his first love. Sweet Alicia married Aaron here, whom I personally think the world of, and the rest is history. Resentment? Yes, definitely! Kidnapping or murder? Definitely not!"

"I appreciate your candor, Miss Thompson. Is there anything or anyone that you think might be a factor in her disappearance?"

"There's one saying that I have found to be universally true whenever an occurrence doesn't seem to make a lot of sense. Our father always said, 'Follow the money trail.'"

"That certainly is advice worth following, Miss Thompson. If I have any more questions that come up, may I call you?"

"Certainly, Aubrey. Feel free to get in touch with me anytime. You too, Aaron. You are welcome here whenever you wish to visit."

"Thank you, Delores. I really mean it. I was a little apprehensive about coming over here today and now I see I shouldn't have been. I'll keep you posted, if we hear anything."

"Do that, Aaron. I'll see you gentlemen to the door."

The two men walked down the stone porch and back out to the car. As they drove down Monument Avenue, Aaron could not help but ask, "What do you think of my sister-in-law?"

"She's quite a hard case, isn't she?"

"Definitely. Did you get anything useful from her?"

"You mean, do I think she's involved? I really don't think so. She's just too open a book. She couldn't hide something if she wanted. Her feelings are written on her face, as they say."

"I'm actually glad. As much as I would like to get a break, I would hate to think that her own sister would despise her this much. Alicia could be a lot to swallow at times, but when you get close to her, she's a very intense, caring person. She has been a wonderful wife and friend to me. I still miss her every minute of the day."

"Well, let's hope we can find her soon."

"I'm beginning to worry that I won't see her again."

"Don't give up hope yet, Aaron. There's a lot going on here and I don't think we've seen the end to this whole process yet. There's not an end point or any closure."

"What sort of closure do you mean?"

"For example, in a robbery, something obviously has to be stolen. In a murder, there would be a body and, generally speaking, some sort of motive no matter how 'far out' it may seem to a rational person. Even in an arson case, you would of course have a fire. So, what do we have in this case? A totally unexplained disappearance. Not a random kidnapping. The chauffeur was professionally executed. The perpetrator knew where to find her and her disappearance has been so clean that the police can track it no farther than the parking lot where it occurred. All too slick, too organized to not have some sort of serious motive. When that becomes clear, and it will, we'll then know where to look and how to proceed. That's why I say I think she's still alive and that there will be contact with the kidnappers before too long."

"That all does make sense. At least I want it to. It gives me some hope."

"I'm not just trying to make you feel better. Understand?"

"I do. Let me ask you a question, Aubrey."

"Ask away."

"What on earth ever prompted you to do this sort of work? I mean, it has to be terribly depressing to be involved in all this debauchery."

"Sometimes it is. Originally, I would have to say I got into this for justice, or maybe it would better serve the truth to call it revenge for my friend Lenny."

"How's that?"

"We were childhood friends. We lived on the same street and grew up together. We were pretty much inseparable. When we weren't in school, we'd go play in the woods together. We built a fort, went skinny dipping, spent entire days fishing with cane poles. You know, all the things young boys did back then. There was an old dirt road and a set of train tracks that ran through our community and they went right through the woods where we hung out. The trains that used those track were normally freight trains and they never went too fast. Sometimes we talked about jumping onto the cars like hobos and going to see the world. Neither of us had ever been out of the town we grew up in, Petersburg, Virginia, just south of here. There's a lot of deep ravines down there and one of them had an old train trestle across it, kinda like an old wooden bridge. It wasn't all that long, maybe a couple dozen yards at the most.

"We got to daring each other to try to cross the ravine on the trestle when we heard the next train whistle. You know kids. It was stupid to say the least. I told Lenny I wasn't afraid and I'd do it in a heartbeat. We bet a dollar on it. So, me being the bravest, or the dumbest depending on your point of view, I took off at a gallop. I'd never crossed the trestle before and didn't realize how high it would be when I got on it. Understand, it was just big wooden timbers and the tracks were laid on top of them. It was open between the planks and you could fall right through if you took a wrong step.

"Once I started across I began to get scared and didn't keep up the speed I needed to beat the train. I heard Lenny screaming at me to hurry. Then I saw the train start out on the trestle and I knew I couldn't make it. In a panic, I dropped between two of the timbers and hung on for dear life. The hundred-year-old beams of the trestle began to shake so bad I didn't think I'd be able to hang on.

The timbers groaned as if they were alive and suffering. Loose gravel from some of the cars poured down on top of me. For just a second I actually thought of just letting go and dropping into the water below. I knew it was shallow and full of rocks and the odds of surviving the hundred-foot drop were nil. I dug my fingers into the wood until I could feel splinters piercing the skin under my nails.

"It seemed like the train took an hour to pass over me. In reality it probably wasn't more than two minutes, tops. Full of adrenalin when the train was gone, I pulled myself back up and went back to where Lenny had been. As I got close to where the trestle started, an old green van was pulling away on the dirt road and there was no Lenny. I searched the woods for an hour. Finally, I figured he must have thought I didn't survive the train passing over me on the trestle and went for help. I headed home, more than a little apprehensive. When I got there, Lenny hadn't returned. I didn't know what to say or think.

"Before long the police came to my house and asked me all kinds of questions. Nothing I said gave them any sort of leads. They put out an APB for the van but that never paid off. I was very depressed without Lenny, mind you, not really eating or sleeping. About two weeks later, I was in school. The principal sent for me and when I got to the office, my mother and the cops were there. They told me that Lenny's body had been found in an old abandoned tobacco barn less than two miles from where I last saw him. His body, what was left of it, was in pieces so small they collected him in garbage bags. They wouldn't tell me much more than that. I read about it in the paper. The paper said he had been kept tied to a timber in the barn and tortured for days. They described the scene as something out of a horror movie.

"For the longest time, I'd go back to the woods and try to force myself to go into the barn. It was very difficult; Lenny and I were like brothers. Finally, one day it started to rain while I was near the barn. I felt like I wanted to go in it and staying dry was the excuse I needed to make myself do it. It was very old and even had a dirt floor. It took me a few minutes to get used to the darkness. When my eyes finally adjusted I could see the large timber in the center of the single room that supported the whole roof. It was not even finished wood. It looked like somebody had just stripped the bark off a tree, cut it the right length and propped it up in the barn to support it. I walked over to it and was jarred when I saw the scratch marks in full circles that went around the timber. The paper said he had been in handcuffs and it was pretty obvious that he had been handcuffed around this piece of lumber. Some of the scratches were deep and were probably made when he was being sliced open and he pulled against the cuffs. It was traumatizing to me just being there. I stayed there, thinking of Lenny and what he must have gone through for days on end until he finally died. I could never bring myself to go back there after that. It's probably still there. God, if we had just gone home that day instead of trying to outrun the train."

"I'm sorry. That is an atrocious thing to have lived through. I can certainly see where that would have given you the drive and incentive to start doing what you do. I'm sure Lenny would be very proud."

"I guess I never really got over it. I wanted to find whoever did that to Lenny and make them pay the ultimate price. They needed to be found, tried, convicted, and electrocuted or hung or shot. Nothing less would be justice. From then on, I just had to understand more about the type of perverts that committed these crimes. I went to the University of Virginia and studied psychology with an emphasis on criminal behavior. Here I am, thirty years or so later. I've made a lot of criminals pay for what was done to Lenny. I'm still committed to it I guess. So that's my story. With any luck, we'll find out who took Alicia and make them pay as well. I want that for you, Aaron."

"I do too, Aubrey. More than I can tell you."

7

Alicia stared at herself in the small mirror that Doctor K had left in the room for her. On first glance, she could not believe her own eyes. If she had not been holding the compact in her hands, she would not have been able to accept that it was her own reflection. Her hair was a butch cut and bleached white. Her features were pale and drawn and the dark circles under her eyes were growing daily. The weight loss had continued until there was literally none left to lose. Her cheeks had become hollow and her skin had a mottled appearance. As she held the mirror up she noticed her arms. There were needle tracks all around the inside of both forearms. The truth was staring her in the face now – she was addicted to heroin in a big way. It was on her mind continually. Her ever increasing need to be under the spell of this narcotic had caused her body to become a human timepiece. As soon as her mind would come out of a stupor, the clock hands would start moving faster and faster. Within an hour of gaining some form of reason, the craving for more would take over and within another hour she would be in excruciating pain if heroin was not forthcoming.

Doctor K was now so confident of the drug's hold on her that he would leave a pack of the white powder, a syringe and a small candle and lighter on the lab bench in her room. Agnes, as she was now responding to readily, no longer resisted the urge to inject herself to find the relief she so desperately required. She had given in completely to whatever her possessor required of her. The only thing that mattered at this point was to stay high, to remain in a heroin-induced state of oblivion. She was in the process of heating a spoonful over the candle when Doctor K entered the room.

"Agnes, my dear, put that away for a while. We're going out for the evening."

She stared at him in disbelief. "Out... I can't... I..."

"Don't be afraid now, Agnes. The world is just the same as when you left it. You're a little different now, but you will be accepted for what you are. Here, put this raincoat on and you'll be fine just as you are. Besides, you've been in here almost two months now. You need a change of environment, you know, to remain a well-rounded individual."

He led her out through the door and into the night. She paid no attention to where she was or her surroundings and followed Doctor K silently, completely malleable to his every touch and command. She had no will of her own. She was a puppet and he was her master. He opened a car door and she sat down on the passenger front seat. Doctor K got behind the wheel and started the engine. As they sped off, she began to plead for a hit. "I need a fix. I need my medicine."

"It's not a medicine, Agnes. It's heroin. It's shit, white blood, not a medicine. Now ask correctly."

"Please, I need some shit. Give me the needle."

"That's better. I don't want your memory putting on any airs, understand? I'll give you a hit in a while. First, you have to go meet some friends of mine. Soon you'll think as much of them as I do. I know that they're going to love you. We'll be there in no time. Try to just lean back and forget about it. You'll get a hit soon enough."

After about ten minutes, which seemed like an eternity to Agnes, the car pulled into an alley behind a row of dirty tenement houses. The alley was full of trash and more than one rat scurried as they got out of the car and made their way to an unmarked door facing the alley. Doctor K knocked several times and a woman, perhaps fifty and very worn looking, answered.

"Vernon, and is this the young lady you've been telling me about?"

"Margaret, this is Agnes. Agnes, this is my good friend, Margaret. Why don't you take Agnes and get her all prettied up, Margaret? I'm sure your other guests would like her to be a little fresher than she is right now."

"My God, Vernon, she smells like a field-hand. Why don't you get her to a washroom once in a while?"

"She has other, more pressing needs than soap and water, Margaret."

"A hop-head, huh?"

"I'm afraid so. I've tried to rehabilitate her, but the pull of the monkey has just been too much for her."

As Margaret grabbed her arm and tried to help her down the hall to the bathroom, Agnes kept repeating, "I need a fix. For God's sake, somebody... I need the needle. Please help me, Margaret. Please!"

"I don't know about this, Vernon. You didn't tell me she would be this strung out."

"Relax, Margaret. If she wasn't on dope, she wouldn't have anything to do with the group you're handing her over to. I'm sure the bulk of them will be so drunk they won't even know she's alive. Here, give her the needle and she'll calm down."

He handed it to Margaret and she took it and Agnes into the small dirty bathroom. After fifteen or so minutes, she escorted the now high Agnes into a bar-like area where Doctor K sat with a group of unsavory looking characters. Agnes was now wearing a negligee, cheap fake jewelry and a heavy dose of overwhelmingly strong perfume. The dark circles under her eyes had been covered with pancake makeup and her lips painted a bright red. She was the stereotypical bar-fly to all those present. For herself, she had no idea where she was and could care less. Doctor K walked over to her with a fat, middle-aged man that looked as if he had just crawled out of the cab of a tractor-trailer. He rubbed the hair on his belly through the gap in his un-tucked shirt as he looked Agnes over. He drew a deep drag from his unfiltered Camel and blew the spoke into her face. He reached out and touched her breast. Agnes gave no response or even acknowledgement of his presence.

"So this is the little woman, huh, Vernon? She ain't much to look at."

He took his large, crusty hand and squeezed her jaw as if examining a horse. "She ain't worth fifty dollars. I'll give you twenty."

"You drive a hard bargain, Phil. But since we're friends, she's all yours. There's a room just behind that door to the right there. Remember now, there are others waiting, so don't keep her all night."

"This won't take long. Come with me, bitch."

He took Agnes' hand and led her effortlessly to the room. Doctor K joined several others that could have been the trucker's twin brothers back at a table where they were all devouring pitcher after pitcher of beer. Phil returned in about fifteen minutes, smiling from ear to ear, exposing a mal-arranged display of yellow and black teeth. He sat down with the group, all of whom laughed at the shit-eating grin on his face. He took a hard swallow of beer, spilling as much on his chest as he drank and announced to the group, "Next!"

They all doubled over with drunken laughter and the clone to his right stood up, handed twenty dollars to Doctor K. "Alright, Vernon. I'm up."

After each was finished with her, the next would go back into the room and take his turn. Doctor K., a/k/a Vernon, who could care less what any man had paid, sold her for as little as five dollars. With one, a tattoo artist who pleaded poverty, he agreed to let him have her if he would go to his car, get his tools and tattoo Agnes in several places. Nothing large, just something to help her attain the "right look" for her profession. The deal made, the last piece of Agnes sold and delivered, Vernon retrieved her from the back room. He was pleased to see that she had a fresh, blackened eye, a split lip that needed a stitch or two and a front tooth missing. To complete her new look, he had the bartered tattoos installed as he watched. A small, red, rose was dutifully inlaid on her left cheek, right under the cheekbone, and a serpent in a bush that more closely resembled a vagina, was needled onto the top of her left breast.

"Beautiful, they're just beautiful. Can you come back another night and do some more for me?"

"Sure man, beats paying for pussy. I'll be back on the weekend."

As the hour was very late, the patrons and Vernon's customers began to leave. After the last had gone, he put his arm under Agnes, who had not so much as flinched through the whole process and lifted her to her feet. Margaret came over to them.

Vernon reached in his pocket and pulled out all the money he had bargained for Agnes.

"Here, take this. We just came for a good time."

"I don't know about this woman, Vernon. She looks to me like she needs to be in a hospital. She's close to OD'ing right now."

"She'll be fine. I'll get her in bed and she'll just sleep it off. Now, I trust that our little arrangement here is still just between us."

"Of course, I know how to keep my mouth shut."

"Good. We'll be back soon. Goodnight, Margaret."

Vernon loaded Agnes into the car and carted her back to the waiting lab room where she had spent the past two months. He laid her on the bed, cut off the lights, and locked the door as he left her room. She would be out until her body clock woke up for its next feeding. By this point, death would be a welcome reprieve from the living hell where she resided.

8

Six months had passed since Aaron Goldman had last seen his wife. No arrests had been made, no leads had been ignored, and no body had been found. The trauma had found its way into his business affairs as well as his personal life. For all practical purposes, Fred Burns had run the business through the early days of Alicia's abduction. It was obvious to all involved that large blocks of stocks were being purchased and that could only mean one thing, Aaron's rivals would soon be making an attempt to dethrone him from the chairmanship of the company.

Aaron threw himself back into the business in an attempt to divert his mind from the trauma that lay just beneath the surface of his psyche. There were those at the company that were glad and others who were disappointed by his reemergence. The power he had so tightly maintained over the years had been allocated to a number of others, most notably Fred Burns. Many new schemes would be set aside because of his reappearance.

At the suggestion of Freda Payne, he decided to attend a group meeting of others who had lost a member of their immediate family to violence. The gathering was held each week at a church not far from Virginia Industrial so he made arrangements to attend.

There were about twenty-five people in the room including the mediator. Cooper was a clinical psychologist who specialized in therapy for those suffering bereavement and its ensuing depression. He felt that this sort of group therapy offered the best approach for helping people work through their loss.

"Welcome everyone! We have a couple of guests with us tonight. Rather than have them be formally embarrassed, why don't we all just introduce ourselves informally before we get started. We have Janet Margolis and Aaron Goldman here tonight. Let's all get a soda off the refreshment table and take ten before we call the meeting to order. According to plan, almost everyone came over to the two new attendees and introduced themselves. There was one particularly friendly young woman in the group who remained after the rest had gone on to chat with the regulars that were present.

"So, you're Aaron Goldman. Virginia Industrial, right?"

"That's right. How did you know?"

"My father, Archie Williams, worked for you up until he retired a couple years ago. Do you remember him?"

Aaron truly didn't recognize the name, but such a situation had arisen before and he was quite experienced at recognizing the accomplishments of employees he had never met.

"Archie Williams. Absolutely. So he's your father. It's obvious that he did as good a job at home raising a family as he did with us. And your name is?"

"Joan. Joan Williams. Nice to meet you, Mr. Goldman. My father always loved working for you. He said you were fair to your employees."

"Call me Aaron, please. Why do you come to these meetings, Joan?"

"My mother was killed by a hit and run driver just a few months ago. I'm having a hard time dealing with it. We were more like sisters and I guess I just need help in getting on with my life. I thought meeting other people who had had a similar experience might help. You're here because of your wife, right?"

"Yes. You heard about the kidnapping?"

"Who didn't? It's been on the news for months. Still no arrests?"

"No. And the police don't seem to be making any real progress. It's been very frustrating. Especially the not knowing. I've worried myself sick over it. I hoped coming here might help."

"Well, let's help each other. I think they're getting ready to start the meeting. Come sit by me."

It made Aaron feel good to have the attention of this young woman. She offered something that had been missing in his life since Alicia's disappearance. Throughout the series of testimonials and heart-wrenching tales, they kept turning to look at one another. There was an immediate mutual attraction. By the time the meeting had adjourned, they both had the same thought. Aaron spoke first.

"Would you like to go get a coffee or snack of some sort with me? The plant is just down the road. I can have someone in security drive your car home for you and it will be there by the time we eat and I drive you home. What do you say?"

"If you're willing to go to that much trouble for me, how could I possibly say no?"

They left together and drove to a small diner that stayed open all night where Aaron had spent many evenings thinking things over during the past few months. A steady, cold winter rain had begun falling, so Aaron took off his jacket and held it over both of their heads as they ran inside. The inclement weather had brought a number of others there and it was a noisy, yet warm atmosphere. The smell of late night bacon and fresh coffee was overpowering. Aaron and Joan found a booth near the rear and sat across from each other.

"This place is wonderful, Aaron. I've driven past it for years, but I never came in before. I guess I'm just part of the McDonald's generation. It's either hamburgers and fries or tacos."

"Joan, how old are you? I don't want anyone to think I'm a dirty old man."

"Don't be silly. I'm twenty-six and on my own. And you?"

"Me?"

"Yeah, tell me a little about Aaron Goldman, the successful industrialist."

"There's really nothing that special about me. I'm thirty-seven, been married to Alicia for over fifteen years and I have to admit, we had a nice, quiet, happy existence up until six months ago. My whole world was fractured when she disappeared. I think I'm a little better now. I still wake up some mornings and think that she's in the bed beside me. It's pretty depressing when that occurs. It's kind of like it happens all over again, my first hearing that she had been taken. I wouldn't wish this on anyone. It's not knowing what happened to her... Sometimes I think it would be better if..."

"If?"

"Well, if they found her body and I knew it was over. I could at least get on with my life. The way it is right now, it's like an unending nightmare, just waiting to hear something."

Joan reached over and lightly touched Aaron's hand. "I can't imagine how bad that must be to live with. Listen, anytime you feel like talking to someone about it, I'm here."

"You're very thoughtful."

"All this time since the kidnapping. No leads? No clues? I always believed that the police eventually solved almost every crime. Maybe I watch too many cop shows.

"I feel they have really tried. There's a detective named Freda Payne who still calls every week or so. At least until the last few weeks. I think they're even beginning to lose hope and are… maybe a little embarrassed over not being able to solve this. There is one guy though, a private detective. Aubrey Pryor's his name. He assures me every time I talk with him that he will put it all together. He's supposed to come by the office in the morning and update me on how he's doing with the investigation."

"You have to pay a private investigator, right?"

"Yeah, I've paid him a small fortune over the past few months. With expenses, over forty thousand dollars."

"Jesus, I didn't know they made that kind of money. Wonder why anyone would remain a regular cop if they could do that well on their own?"

"Most of them probably don't do that well. He's supposed to be the best in the business. At least around here. Was with the FBI for a long time. He is a peculiar duck, though."

"How's that?"

"He never seems to ask the questions that you're expecting. It's like he's way out in left field and yet, when he fixes on a person, he's as good as you have ever seen at figuring out where people are coming from. I wouldn't have kept paying him this long with so little success if I didn't think he might really come up with an answer. If he can't do it, I just don't believe anyone can."

"I'm sure it'll work out, Aaron."

She touched his hand again, this time letting hers remain for a little longer than the first time. Even Aaron, who had never considered himself much of a ladies' man, was aware that she was interested in him, and more than just his friendship. After another hour of small talk, he drove her to her small apartment and walked her to the door.

"Thank you for letting me spend a little time with you. I had a great time. When will we do this again? Soon, I hope."

"I had a really nice time, Joan. How about on the weekend we go out? You know, maybe to a show or just out to nice restaurant?"

Joan kissed him quickly on the cheek. "Call me. 'Night, Aaron."

"Goodnight."

As he drove back to his own home, he felt his spirit rise as it hadn't in a long time. He was also aware of a nagging feeling of guilt for even allowing himself to enjoy a woman's company with Alicia's disappearance still unresolved. Maybe it was time to just let go."

* * *

Aubrey Pryor was standing by the receptionist at Virginia Industrial when Aaron arrived. Coffee in hand, he was making notes and talking quietly to himself. He jumped when Aaron spoke to him, causing his coffee to pour over the cup rim and onto the carpet.

"I'm sorry, Aubrey… Didn't mean to startle you."

"My fault, I wasn't paying attention."

"Let me grab a coffee. You want a refill? We can just sit down in the lounge and talk if you want."

"I think we need to talk privately this time, maybe in your office if that's okay."

A little taken aback by the implication that Aubrey may have some information this time, Aaron replied, "Of course, Aubrey. That's fine. Let's go there now."

They seated themselves in Aaron's office. Aaron cleared a spot among all of the papers requiring his attention that had been left by his secretary.

"Tell me that you have uncovered something that will bring all of this to an end."

"Not exactly, Mr. Goldman. Let me ask you a question if I might."

"You know you can always ask me anything."

"Are you aware that a Mr. Ernest Pearlman has his own private investigator asking a lot of questions about you? It's been going on for quite some time."

"How do you know?"

"That's what you pay me for. We have both been interested in talking to the same people. You ask people touchy questions once, they're curious. When other people ask the same question, they get nervous, sometimes offended. Turns out I know the guy he's got working for him. Used to be with Central Intelligence. He's good. Not an inexpensive undertaking either. What interest would he have in finding Mrs. Goldman?"

"He would be more interested in trying to find some dirt on me. He's my main opposition on the Board of Directors here at the company. He'd love nothing better than to be able to drag me through the mud and convince the other members of the board to elect him as the CEO."

Aubrey pushed his glasses up on his nose and squinted as he asked Aaron, "He's not going to find anything that you haven't told me about, is he?"

"I'm an open book, Aubrey. Let his man ask away. I hope that if he should uncover anything about Alicia, he'll share that with us. I doubt it though. He's a particularly nasty individual. A bottom line kind of guy. You know the type?"

"Say no more. I'll stay in touch with his investigator and let him know your concern. If he uncovered something, I'm sure you'd make it worth his while to tell us?"

"Definitely. Now, anything else going on? I hate to tell you this, Aubrey, but you're bound to be aware that a great deal of time and money has already been spent with very little success and I'm considering just trying to get on with my life and put this behind me. Maybe, if something, some fact or evidence of any kind were found, we could start back up, but right now I think you must have a more interesting case than this to go to."

"To be honest with you, Mr. Goldman, you lasted longer than I thought you would. I know that we've hit a lot of dead ends in this one, but whether or not I'm on the payroll, I never give up. It's not my nature. With your permission, I'll keep this going at my own pace and if something breaks, we can put it back in high gear. At this point, the money doesn't mean much to me. You've invested enough already. Don't think I've given up though."

"Sounds like a good arrangement to me, Aubrey. I have been very impressed with your thoroughness in this and that makes me feel that I've done all that I could to find Alicia. Truth is, I'm beginning to feel that she will never turn up. I hate to say it, but I truly believe she's dead. I wish I didn't feel that way, but I do."

"I understand, Mr. Goldman. I'd better let you get back to work now. I'll see myself out."

Aubrey set his coffee cup on the edge of Aaron's desk and turned to leave. Almost as an afterthought, he asked, "That Miss Williams seems like a nice young woman, doesn't she?"

Totally floored by his remark, Aaron only replied, "Yes, she really does."

Aaron watched as Aubrey walked out of the office and disappeared down the hall.

9

Agnes sat upright in the straight-backed chair in her room. A full six months with Doctor K had resulted in a transformation so complete and bizarre that no one who had not witnessed it would have believed it possible. The educated, beautiful, sophisticated woman of society had been reduced to the lowest form of human existence. Not only did she have the physical attributes of a street whore and addict, her very soul had been reduced to the point that she felt correct in her new role. Her once lovely face had aged dramatically. Her features had been twisted by the scars inflicted during her continuous liaisons with the gutter life that used her services as a prostitute. Her need for heroin was now so great that her own physical being was of no value to her other than as a receptacle for the drug that was her existence. Her hair was still a mix of bleached blond and dark roots. It was seldom combed and almost never washed. She would only apply the cheap, pancake makeup and extreme red lipstick and nail polish prior to servicing the johns that Doctor K required before supplying her with heroin. And, the once health-conscious Alicia, now lived with a cigarette in her mouth and a whiskey bottle close by. The stale smell of liquor that she had chided Morris for on that last morning's ride to the auction stayed with her now continually. The veins in her arms had been penetrated so continually by hypodermics that they no longer supported themselves and had collapsed to the point where she had resorted to injecting herself under her toenails and in her calves. Doctor K delighted in his creation. To make sure that even her thought process, or whatever remained of it, was properly in tune with her daily reality, she was fed a diet of pornographic videos and magazines. She seldom witnessed anything in one of the disgusting productions or skin books that she had not already performed for a paying customer in the back room of some seedy motel or bar. Thoughts of her own past never crossed her mind. The most prevalent observation of her existence was now the passage of time that brought with it the next shot of heroin. Doctor K entered the room and walked over to Agnes. Wearing only a pair of skin-tight leather pants, she sat cross-legged in the chair, thumbing subconsciously through a magazine showing young girls engaged in every possible sexual act with middle-aged men.

"Here, darling, have a shot?"

He poured her a large shot of straight whiskey and handed it to her. She downed it in one quick swallow. She took an exaggerated draw from her cigarette. "I'm almost out of shit. You said you would bring it. Where the hell is it? You aren't worth a damn. Why don't you come over here and let Agnes take care of you? Give me your prick and I'll make you feel real good. I'm good with a cock, baby. I just need a little shit, baby. Come on now. I need you, baby. Please, give me some shit. What fucking good are you anyway?"

"First, I wouldn't fuck a sleazy whore like you on a bet. You've been had by a thousand truckers in the past few months and I have no doubt that your once sweet little pussy is now a breeding grounding for the worst that man has to offer in the way of disease. And it's so unfortunate that you have picked this evening to start calling me foul names. After all, Agnes, this is our last evening together."

"You going somewhere? Leave me some dope if you go, man. You fucking promised!"

"I'm not going anywhere, darling. You are."

"Not without a fix. I ain't going no-fuckin-where."

"Oh, yes, you are." He took an overnight bag from under the lab bench and threw it at her. "Put all your stuff in the bag. NOW!"

The tone of his voice got Agnes moving quickly. She knew not to cross him.

"You are complete. As my creation, I cannot improve upon you. It's time to see if you can swim on your own. Now get your stuff and let's go. We've got a long drive ahead of us."

Agnes sat quietly and in a sullen mood in the car. Even though she had been living in hell for six months, it had become her hell and her intellect and instinct had been reduced to the minimum that was required to survive there. Any change would be traumatic to her now. Her world was small and its focus narrowly set on the point of a needle. Like a child being punished, she refused to say a word as the night's ride unfolded. After several hours, they arrived in a small town. With its tight rows of worn shops centered on either side of one long street, it could pass for a town in an old western movie. It was late and only the sparse, dim street lights gave any illumination to the street. A glow at the far end emanated from a series of side street bars servicing the oil workers that dominated the population there. The black ooze they lived in all day never came out of their skin or clothes completely and a smell akin to an unkempt service station permeated the air around that entire end of town. Even a woman as nasty as Agnes would be in demand in such an environment. Doctor K pushed her up the street toward a bar at the far end. The neon sign in front flashed "GANDY DANCER." They were greeted at the door by a robust black man who served as doorman and bouncer. Doctor K spoke to him and he pointed to a door beside the men's room. Dragging Agnes behind him, he entered.

"Danny, my man! I've brought the young woman by I was telling you about."

It seemed that no matter the nature and intellect of those he conversed with, Doctor K could adjust his vocabulary and attitude to mesh.

"That's a woman, huh? She looks like you freed her from a prisoner of war compound."

"She cleans up nice. Knows how to please the men and only requires a little sustenance from you. Give her what she needs and she'll do anything to please. Anything."

"I don't know, Kale. Don't get me wrong. None of the whores I work is what you would call a model citizen but this one looks ten years down the road of any of them. You know my girls are known for their classy looks, man."

"Why not use her for the johns that the other women have a problem with."

"I'll tell you what, I'll try her for a few days but I ain't gonna promise to take her on 'til I see that she can produce. After all, I'm running a business here; this ain't a soup kitchen."

"Fair enough. Okay, Agnes, this is your new owner. He'll take care of you and your needs from here on out."

As disgusting and painful as her association with Doctor K had been, she grabbed ahold of his arm tightly, not wanting to let go of the only security left in her life. She was no longer even a shadow of the beautiful, aristocratic woman who had confidently mixed with the highest levels of society less than a year earlier. No one who knew her then would believe what she had become. None would even recognize her."

"Get your hands off me." Doctor K pushed her toward the pimp he had given her to.

"It's not the end of the world, darling. There's other women here. You'll make friends and meet a lot more men."

Doctor K was disgusted by Danny's show of concern. "Hell, Danny, she's used to eight or ten men a night. She doesn't care, white, black, old, young, mean or half dead, she'll service them all for you. Well, I gotta get going, I'll check on her in a few weeks. I've grown rather fond of her and have a little curiosity about where she goes from here. I'll be in touch."

He turned and walked back out into the night, leaving Agnes with Danny the pimp and a new prison to get accustomed to. Danny called out to another girl who prostituted for him, "Mary Lou! Get your ass in here!" A hard looking and over-painted young woman entered the room and stood in front of Danny. In her late thirties, the overweight but well-endowed black woman half sneered as she looked at her handler, and asked, "Yeah, Danny. What's up?"

"See this pathetic looking bitch?"

"Yeah. So what? You working street people now? What is this? 'Will screw for food'?"

"Just shut the fuck up. I want you to get her cleaned up and let me look at her. She'll stay with you a few days 'til I see if she works out. And Mary Lou…"

"What?"

"I think you need to back her off the mule some, if you can. She's too strung out to even stand up straight. If she can't hold back some, she won't be alive in six weeks. And don't let her handle any money or deal with street pushers. If she gets any shit, it comes from me. Got it?"

"I can hear. This her bag?"

"Yeah. Now get her out of here."

Mary Lou grabbed Agnes around the waist and picked up her bag. "All right, woman, help me some, will you? I ain't carryin' you. My back gets enough exercise already. I slip a disc or pinch a nerve and I'll be on the streets myself and that ain't never happenin' again. That's it. Just keep walking."

They left Danny shaking his head in doubt about whether his new acquisition would be of any value to him at all.

Mary Lou had a room over the bar as did several of the other women that worked there. It was not only her insulation from the world outside but somewhat of a status symbol among the group she worked with. Here was a woman who Danny thought enough of to furnish a place of her own. She realized that her arrangement with him was in fact bargaining with the devil, but from where she had come, it was a step up. At least she was self-sufficient and had this small room to call home. She was not enthralled over the prospect of sharing it with some poor white trash Danny had picked up from the gutter.

Still, Mary Lou did not have to remember that far back to see herself as the battered and impoverished woman that had arrived at this same spot a few short years earlier. This woman was close to the end of her rope unless someone helped her. Mary Lou fully understood that a lot of people wound up that way because of personal flaws that would never change in spite of any help they were given. To get involved with such a hard case could be the most frustrating and hopeless undertaking anyone might attempt.

She would wade in slowly and test the water before getting in over her head. She had enough problems of her own.

"All right. Come on, girl. Let's see can we get you cleaned up."

"I need a hit. Can you get me a fix? I'm hurting... Bad."

"You come with me and take a shower and I'll see what I can do. Now, I ain't in no mood to put up with a bunch of shit. You want help, you do what I say. Got it?"

Offering no response or resistance, Agnes took the hand being offered and followed Mary Lou to the old black and white ceramic tile, shared bathroom at the end of the hall. Whatever in the way of bathing she'd had during her stay with Doctor K had been out of a wash pan. The hot shower felt better than she could even have imagined. It was the first human compassion that anyone had shown her for many months. Even though there was a grinding in her stomach and her mind was begging for the drug that numbed it from the world, she lingered under the stream of steaming hot water. Mary Lou had to make her get out.

"Woman, you gonna shrivel up and go down the drain. You can shower whenever you want to. But right now Danny wants me to make you presentable, so we got to find something to make you look pretty. God knows that ain't gonna be none too easy. Good Lord, I don't believe I ever seen anybody with as many tracks as you got on your arms. You got to slow down on that shit. You just looking for one bad hit to kill you, girl!"

She stared into Agnes' worn face. "How did you get so many little scars on your face? You don't have to answer that. I can imagine. Some big, tough guy proving to you just how macho he was... Am I right? I seen my share of that type. But no more. Anybody try to hurt me now and Danny will bust their ass. He ain't the best kind of man but at least he don't beat on women. And that's a big thing with me. You hear me girl? You listening to anything I'm saying?"

Surprisingly, Agnes nodded.

"Good. Now we're getting somewhere. Throw this towel around you and let's see if you have anything to wear in your bag."

A quick glance inside was all she needed. "Damn, we need to burn these things. I don't even want them in my room. I swear, there's things in there I ain't never smelled the likes of before."

She took the entire bag over to her lone window, opened it and tossed the torn bag and its contents into the alley to takes its place with the other piles of garbage. "I'll find you something to wear. Anything would be better than what you had. Here, put on these."

She tossed a bra and a pair of panties to her and Agnes dropped her towel and put them on.

"Here, this little number might fit you. You ain't nothing but a skeleton, but it's way too small for me so maybe it'll work."

She helped Agnes pull the dress on over her head. "That ain't half bad. We'll do you right, yet. Now, let's work on that hair some and try a little makeup. Maybe Danny will keep you when I get done with you."

It was not hard to make Agnes' appearance remarkably better. When Mary Lou finished with her, she stood back and admired the improvement. "Uh-uh! Don't even look like the same woman."

Agnes was beginning to burn inside. "I really need some shit. Can't you help me? I gotta have a hit."

"Let's go see Danny. He wants to take a look at you and he's the only one here that's going to have what you need. I tell you what though, babe, you better ease up on that stuff."

Mary Lou bent over and kissed her gently on the forehead. "You look real nice now. Let's go see the boss."

The bar was beginning to show signs of life as the first oil workers to get off work were just arriving. Danny was sitting between two of the regulars, buying them a couple of rounds to get them started. He knew that if they got a buzz on, they would stay until their pockets were empty. A dozen rounds and a quick trick with one of Danny's whores was generally all it took. He saw Mary Lou and Agnes approaching. "That the same girl, Mary Lou?"

"It is."

"Damn, you're good. You should be working with those designer guys that have the broads go down that walkway with the thousand dollar dresses on. No shit, she could be a keeper now."

"Good. Now, what are you gonna do about getting her a fix? She's in bad shape."

"I can help her out, but I'm putting you in charge of backing her off this shit some, Mary Lou. I don't want her stoned around the clock. You keep track of when she gets high and don't let anybody else get her anything. You think you can do that?"

"I don't mind helping her out."

"Good. Bring her over here and I'll get her a little relief for now. I'm gonna start tapering down on your hits though, girl. Your name's Agnes?"

Agnes fixed her eyes on the needle being prepared and did not respond.

* * *

Freda Payne opened the meeting in the conference room of the Henrico County Sheriff's Department. This was to be the final full department wrap up of the investigation into Alicia's disappearance. "I'm sorry to have to say that the few leads we had in this case have pretty much turned out to be dead-ends. No ransom demands have been made; no motives offered; and no witnesses. What with the heavy caseloads we all have, I hate to say this, but we're going to have to put the Goldman case on the back burner unless there's a breakthrough of some sort. Does anyone here have any new information or leads that have not been followed up on yet?"

There was no response.

"Aubrey Pryor is here this morning. I'm sure most of you know him. Aubrey, how are things from your end? Have you broken any new ground?"

Aubrey slowly looked up from his notepad. "Nope, but I have not given up and as you know, my persistence usually produces results, no matter how far down the road that may be. I will, I repeat, I will get to the bottom of Alicia Goldman's kidnapping. I would like to spend a little time with each member of the investigating team before you start filing away your notes. I want to make sure I have information on every single lead that has been checked out. No matter how unimportant they might seem, I want to know every last detail. I'll meet with each of you as your time permits. And, of course, I'm always available if something breaks. Detective Payne has my numbers. Call anytime, day or night."

"Thanks, Aubrey, we all appreciate your efforts. Anybody else?"

No response.

"That's pretty much the story. How about the pay phone? Thurman, were there ever any more calls placed to the Goldman house from that location?"

"No, ma'am. The surveillance teams stopped watching the booth some time back and there have been no contacts made from there through today. If you don't mind though, I'm going to put a receiving unit at the Goldman house that will intercept any calls from that number and transmit the call right here to one of a bank of hot lines phones I have set up in the communications room. If anyone calls his house from there, someone from our group will alert a patrol car in a matter of seconds. Also, I am still cross-matching phone records from all of the employees at Mr. Goldman's company to see if anyone there has made or received calls from that number.

Aubrey, a sparkle suddenly showing in his eyes, directed a question to the young computer protégé. "This cross-checking you're doing...

"Yes, sir?"

"What sort of information are you looking for? How do you know what's of importance to the case?"

"Without computers, of course, this would be completely impossible. However, with the new database search engines, we can cross-check literally thousands of individual phone numbers and see who has been calling who and when. So, if on a specific date and at a specific time, an incident of some importance to a particular case occurred, for example, the actual abduction of Mrs. Goldman, we can see if there was any flurry of calls between any two individuals that appear to be in some way affected by the time. Do you see what I'm driving at here?"

"Very ingenious. I am impressed. You will of course advise me if you uncover any information relevant to Mrs. Goldman's disappearance, won't you?"

"Absolutely!"

"Like I said, there's nothing concrete as of yet. I'm just looking for any suspicious calling patterns or even calls made at odd times. Once in a while, this produces some unusual results that create new leads. I'll keep you posted."

"Thanks, Thurman. Well, let's all get back to work, but do touch base on this one from time to time as there has to be more to it than we've seen so far. Good day."

10

Agnes was responding to her environment. For the most part, as long as the women at the Gandy Dancer performed as required for Danny and gave him the proceeds, the remainder of their time was their own. Mary Lou had accepted the challenge of bringing Agnes back into the realm of the living. She had been personally handling her fixes with Danny's blessings. Every week she would reduce the amount of heroin by about ten percent. Agnes' periods of being lucid were growing longer and she didn't seem to notice that the drug had been reduced in strength. Her gentleness and sympathy also resulted in Agnes offering no resistance to Mary Lou's sexual advances. Like many prostitutes, Mary Lou had lost any attraction to men. She considered them johns with a paycheck for her and that was it. She didn't seem to be bothered by the fact that Agnes' ability to rationalize her actions was non-existent. Besides, without her, Agnes would have been dead, she reasoned. Agnes was now as dependent on Mary Lou as she had been on the mad doctor. It was nonetheless a surprise when one evening after sending the last customers packing and she and Agnes sat on the bed having a nightcap of warm beer, Agnes began to undergo a period of clarity that Mary Lou was totally unprepared for.

"Alicia."

"What, babe?"

"Alicia. I'm Alicia."

"You mean, Agnes, sweetheart. Your name is Agnes."

"No… It's not. My name is not Agnes. Doctor K wanted me to be Agnes. I'm Alicia."

"Okay. I'll bite. Where are you from, Alicia? Do you have a family?"

"I did. But no more. They're all dead now."

"Dead? How did they die?"

"Doctor K killed them all. They're dead."

"This Doctor K. He's the guy who brought you here?"

"He gave me to Danny. He owned me and so he just gave me to him."

"Sweetheart, there ain't nobody who owns you. We're gonna get your head on straight before long and figure what all this is about. What was your last name? Did you have a husband or a lover? Kids?"

As quick as the lucid moment came, it disappeared. "I need a hit. Have you got some shit?"

"Talk to me a little more, baby. What was the rest of your name? Alicia what?"

"God damn it! I need a hit. I'm hurting. Please, give me some. You take care of me and I'll make you feel real good, Mary Lou. You know I can. I'm so very good to you. I'll kiss you everywhere that you love. Won't you get me a hit now?"

She eased over beside Mary Lou and started stroking her cheek. "Agnes will treat you good, real good. I just need a little shit, baby."

Mary Lou took her hand, pulled it down and kissed it gently. "I'll get you a hit. Tomorrow we'll talk some more."

The next few days produced more signs of a reemerging intellect and Mary Lou was excited that her efforts were producing results. It was also pleasing to her that Alicia, as she was now calling her, responded ever more aggressively to her sexual advances. She had learned that only a year earlier, the mere thought of embracing another woman would have been revolting to Alicia. After all, it had even ruined her relationship with her sister Delores. Back then it had seemed morally wrong and personally despicable. Mary Lou was convinced that any other secrets Alicia had locked up inside would soon be forthcoming.

* * *

It was late and only a few patrons remained at the Gandy Dancer when Doctor K entered. He immediately spotted Alicia at a rear booth with Mary Lou.

"Ladies, how good to see you. Goodness, Agnes, you certainly look comfortable with your new life."

Alicia slid close beside Mary Lou and recoiled away from him.

"Now, that's not very hospitable."

Feeling a little braver with Mary Lou beside her, she responded in a way that caught Doctor K off guard. "Go away! I'm Alicia. I'm Alicia. Agnes is gone. I'm Alicia. Make him leave, Mary Lou."

"Don't worry, baby, I won't let him hurt you. She doesn't want to see you. Why don't you leave us alone?"

"Young lady, when I get to the point in my life where I need to take any advice from a street whore, I'll be sure and look you up. Until then, you'll shut the fuck up 'til you're spoken to. I hope you understand where I'm coming from."

The maniac behind his eyes was readily apparent to her. "No, I don't, but I do know where you're going. Danny... Danny, can you come here?"

Within seconds Danny, used to responding to calls for assistance and dealing with unruly customers who often got rough with his girls, came over to see what was happening.

"Kale. What's happening?"

"Nothing, Danny. I was just in the area and dropped by to see how the little urchin that I brought to you was getting along. I'm shocked that she has forgotten my kindness. I guess it's true what they say about no good deed going unpunished. And her friend here, she's downright hostile. What have I ever done to deserve such abusive behavior?"

Danny sensed the hostility toward Kale and his sarcasm pointed out that he was instigating the situation. "Why don't you let me get you a cold beer, Kale? Come on over and sit with me. The girls were just leaving anyway. You can see that the girl is doing a lot better. Mary Lou there has kinda taken her under her wing and she's coming round."

"I can see that. However, I think you may find that a whore without a strong thought process is a lot easier to deal with than a philosopher such as Agnes' new custodian there."

There was now a studied look on his face. "I can't stay. I just wanted to see how she was doing. Obviously, she's fine. I'll be going."

He left as quickly as he had entered. Mary Lou and Alicia went over to where Danny stood. She hugged him quickly. "Thanks, Danny. What a creepy guy. I think he's a lot of what's wrong with Alicia. There's no telling what he was doing to her while she stayed with him. He makes the guys who come in here look like preachers. He's so small and safe looking. Goes to show you, you never know who to trust. We're going to bed now. 'Night love."

"See you tomorrow, ladies."

* * *

Friday night was always the busiest night of the week at the Gandy Dancer. The oil workers had gotten paid and could barely wait to get to a bar, have a few beers, and find a woman to hit on.

They were a loud, rough, unmannered group, but for the most part, they were good natured. At the Gandy Dancer, fights were rare, When they did occur, Danny and the bartender Albert handled them expertly. The instigators would be shown the door and they would be forgiven by the next night. They were in the business of showing people a good time. They weren't a police station.

The usual crowd was there and the music was blaring out the front door by 11 p.m. Most of the girls were working on their fourth trick of the evening. No one paid any particular attention to the guy at one end of the bar who quietly surveyed the crowd. His dark complexion, sunglasses and hat all but hid his features and a dark mustache finished the mask. He was slim and angular and in obvious concentration unrelated to the festivities surrounding him.

After a few beers, he took his glass of dark draft and walked slowly around the club, sizing up the patrons. He approached several girls and eventually wound up sitting in a booth with Mary Lou.

"Haven't seen you in here before. New on the rigs?"

"How'd you know?"

"Normally I can smell the oil on everybody. After a few months, you can wash as much as you want, but it stays with you. Eventually all the men wind up spending some time with me. I'm the best woman in the bunch. You want a woman, don't you?"

"Maybe. How much?"

"Depends what want me to do."

"Everything… The works."

"Fifty bucks. Anything you want but for only an hour. Meter's running. What d'you say?"

"Who's that girl over there with white hair? I think I know her from somewhere?"

"I doubt it. That's Alicia. She's not quite all there upstairs, if you know what I mean. Sweet, but not a lot of gray matter. You need me, sweetheart. Let's go upstairs together. You on?"

"Sounds good to me, but let me get a closer look at... Alicia you called her?"

"Yeah. Okay, but make it quick. The clock's started."

They walked over to where Alicia was standing beside a young man negotiating for her services. Her limited ability to handle any dickering over price always resulted in the same response from her. "Thirty bucks."

No matter how many times they asked for a break, the reply was always, "Thirty bucks."

Mary Lou's new john stood in front of Alicia. "I know you. You're the bitch that stole my wallet in Phoenix. I thought you looked familiar. I want my money back, you thieving whore!"

"I didn't steal nothin' from you. I didn't. Ask Mary Lou. She'll tell you. I don't even count the money. I..."

With no warning, he smacked her face fiercely with the back of his hand. The young man with her pushed him away. "Hey man, you don't hit her. She's with me."

Mary Lou reacted quickly. "Danny! Danny! Get over here!"

As Danny and Albert responded to her request for help, the agitated accuser drew a pistol from under his belt. He directed his aim dead on Alicia's face. As his hand tightened, and only a second away from blowing her face off, Mary Lou grabbed his hand. He turned and directed the first round into her chest. As she fell to the floor, mortally wounded, he re-focused on Alicia and quickly squeezed off two more rounds. She in turn, dropped instantly onto the hard tile, only a few feet from her friend. The gunman fired several other random shots around the room until he was certain that no one was advancing on him. Danny and the bartender had frozen in their tracks. With no one in immediate pursuit, he ran out of the Gandy Dancer, and disappeared into a steady drizzle. The two women lay motionless in a pool of blood and a deathly silence overcame the revelry that had only moments before, filled the room.

11

"Darling, that was incredible. No, don't move. Just stay right on top of me for a while. I'm still having little explosions inside. Mmm... I don't want it to end. You're the best lover I've ever known. My entire body feels like I'm another part of you when you're in me. I feel like I just melted onto your penis. Jesus, it's great."

"Joanie, you're so beautiful. I can't tell you how much you mean to me. I feel like you've brought me back from the dead. After Alicia, I didn't think I'd ever find another woman I could be happy with. Now I know how wrong I was. You make me feel twenty again. You know what I want us to do?"

"So soon? My, you are a stud muffin."

"I wish you... No, I want you to go on a trip with me."

"Really? To where?"

"How about Vegas? We could take the company jet and be there by morning. It's only 10 p.m. I can have my pilot meet us over at the airport and be ready to go in two hours. What do you say?"

"You have a private jet?"

"It belongs to the company, but I decide who gets to use it. I can't think of any better use to put it to. You in?"

"I'm in. Unbelievable. I'm going to Vegas in a private jet."

"I see a lot of trips in your future, young lady."

Joan kissed Aaron firmly and deeply, clasping his chin with both hands as she thrust her tongue deep into his mouth. She finally withdrew to breathe. "I'm in need of some trips right now, with you."

"Okay, get some clothes together pronto. Bring along something sexy to wear out tomorrow evening. We can catch a show."

"One black, skin tight evening dress with a slit clear up to my slit coming up."

"You are one hot woman."

"I'm whatever you want me to be, darling. Give me thirty minutes and I'm ready."

Aaron placed a call to his pilot, waking him from a deep sleep. The jet would be ready when they arrived at the airport.

It was midnight when Aaron and Joan boarded the Gulfstream executive jet. The pilot was already going through his checklist and a stewardess greeted them as they boarded from the last step up the gangplank.

"Good evening, Mr. Goldman. You must be Miss Williams. Welcome aboard. As soon as you are both seated, we'll be leaving. Can I get you something to drink or a snack?"

Aaron smiled at Joan. "How about champagne? I'm certain there's some aboard. Am I right, Andrea?"

"Of course, sir. There's always champagne aboard."

"Bring us a couple of glasses if you would."

"Yes, sir."

Aaron and Joan sat in two large swivel chairs in the custom salon of the jet. The engines began to whine and by the time the champagne arrived, the jet was already beginning to taxi down the runway.

"Aaron, I can't believe we're doing this. It's like I'm a character in a fairy tale. Things like this don't happen for girls like me."

"Obviously, that's no longer true. For you at least. There is no substitute for the best things in life. You've got to grab for them. Nobody gives you anything. You want it; you fight for it. I want you. So I'm putting up a good fight, am I not?"

"You are indeed. When will we get to Vegas?"

"Since we have no stops or connections, we'll be there in about three and half hours. This is a very fast jet. Not to mention we won't have to wait an hour for someone to give us our bags. They're right there in the locker, just in front of the bedroom."

"Bedroom?"

"You didn't know there was a bedroom? I thought we might grab a couple hours of sleep before we get to Sin City."

"I want to see."

"Okay. As soon as we get up to altitude and the pilot tells us it's okay to get up, I'll show it to you. Meanwhile, a toast. To you, to me, to us."

They both downed their glasses. After a couple of minutes, the jet leveled off and Aaron motioned Joan to follow him to the aft cabin. He pushed open the door and with a motion similar to Vanna White showing a contestant the new car they had just won, he pointed out the lovely round, queen sized bed with a black satin cover. Joan was more than impressed. "This is incredible. I had no idea people lived like this. It would be easy to get used to this life."

"Then get used to it."

Aaron sat on the edge of the bed, pulled off his shoes and laid back. As he watched, Joan began rubbing her hands under her breasts and then back up to the top button of her blouse. She slowly freed the first button and continued the fluid movement of her hands over every curve on her luscious body until all the buttons had been freed. She removed the blouse revealing a black French bra of sheer material that clearly showed her erect nipples. She then moved her hands down to the zipper on her tight skirt and, with her fingers turned sideways to allow for use with half-inch pink polished nails, she slid the zipper down and pushed the skirt off her perfectly shaped hips. It moved easily against her silk black half-slip which was a short cut that stopped a full ten inches above her knees. Now wearing only her sexy underwear, she moved purposely over to Aaron and began to kiss him. As he responded, she moved her hands down to his pants. Within seconds, she unzipped his pants and pulled them to the floor. It was obvious from his huge erection that she had his full attention.

"I've never fucked a man in his private jet before."

"I'm glad I'm the first. Now get your beautiful ass up here and let me finish stripping you."

After a round of the most erogenous foreplay Aaron had ever experienced, the sex that followed proved to be of the most extreme nature as well. They both fell into a deep sleep, naked and entwined in each other arms. After what seemed like only minutes of comatose sleep, they were awakened by a soft knock at the cabin door.

"Mr. Goldman, sir. We are on final approach. I thought you would want to know."

"Thank you Andrea. We're awake."

Fifteen minutes later the jet was on the tarmac. Aaron and Joan were met at the General Aviation terminal by a stretch limousine from the Bellagio Hotel and Resort. After a short ride down the Vegas strip, they arrived at the hotel just in time to see the elaborate fountains in the front dancing to the strains of the Boston

Pops." They walked over to a spot in front of the hotel where they could watch the water spouts moving in rhythm with the music.

"Oh, my God, Aaron. This is so beautiful. To be able to be here and see this with you is more than I could ever have wished for. I don't know what I ever did to deserve this moment. It must have been something in a previous life. The lights of the strip, the beautiful hotel, it's all magic to me."

"Don't ever think that you don't deserve this, Joan. For what you've brought to me, this is only a small payment on the account. Now, what do you say we turn in? We'll walk the entire strip tomorrow after breakfast."

"Lead on."

They immediately went to their suite and collapsed again in each other's embrace.

Morning brought a bright desert sun and breakfast in bed. Once again, Aaron was treated to an incredibly erotic performance by Joan as she moved about the lavish suite wearing only a smile. Aaron always admired Alicia for how trim and fit she was, but hers was a look that had remained at its peak thanks to many dollars finding their way into salons. She made the absolute best of the natural gifts she had. But Joan's gift of beauty went far beyond that of any woman he had ever seen. Her skin was like porcelain, her teeth like ivory, and her hair looked like woven silk. She knew she was beautiful and how to use her charms to enthrall a man. Aaron was captivalated. He became sexually aroused practically every time he looked at her. When she laid down beside him, his body was immediately on fire. After breakfast they shared another intimate encounter. They caught their breath, showered together, then went out to see the strip. After visiting a number of the other casinos and resorts, their feet were sore. And Aaron had an idea for another adventure to share.

"Joan, have you ever seen the Grand Canyon?"

"Never. I always wanted to but never thought I'd get the chance. Why?"

"It's only a short helicopter ride from here and there's a place just up the strip where they offer rides to the canyon. What do you say we take one together, right now?"

"Could we? I think that would be just lovely."

As the chopper leaned to the right, Aaron and Joan could pick out the colorful striations on the walls of the canyon. "Oh my God, it's beautiful, Aaron. And, so huge. I could never have imagined anything so, so…"

"How about so 'grand'?"

"That's it exactly."

"Thus the name."

"I see. Very clever. You know, Aaron, you have already shown me more in the short time we've known each other than anyone I've ever spent time with. Your world is so much larger and more beautiful than mine. For that matter, more beautiful than I ever dreamed possible. Please tell me it's not going to end and we don't have to go home."

"Joan, for us it's just starting, darling. There are a million other places I want to show you."

"Such as?"

"How about the islands?"

"You mean Hawaii?"

"Perhaps. I was thinking a little closer to home to start with. The Virgin Islands. They are spectacular with crystal clear water and small mountains rising from the bottom of the ocean. The shores are covered with white beaches and palm trees and the temperature is fabulous year round. Would you like to go there with me, say, next weekend?"

"I'd love to. But I have a job. I'll lose it if I don't go in. I don't have any vacation days."

"So quit your job."

"I'd love to but if I do, I can't pay my rent."

"Why don't you call your boss when we get back to the hotel and tell him that he's fired? Tell him that you no longer have need of his services as your employer. Let me worry about paying your rent. Or perhaps you should move into my big old empty house. It gets pretty quiet and lonely stomping around in that mausoleum. I'd love to have you there with me. What do you say to that?"

"I'm flattered and thrilled, of course. But let me think on it a little. This is all happening so quickly. I love the sound of it but I just don't want to make a mistake that we'll both regret. It's all great now but, like the song says, will you still love me tomorrow."

"Today, tonight and tomorrow."

Aaron kissed her gently as the chopper made its way back to Vegas. As they approached, the strip was illuminated by the millions of lights that make Las Vegas the only city like it in the world.

After returning to the hotel they decided to attend a show at the MGM Grand in the Garden. It was a sold out performance by Luis Miguel but Aaron, using the tried and perfected methods of the very wealthy, procured front row seats only an hour before the show was to start. Undoubtedly, Joan Williams was the most beautiful woman in the entire city that evening. Everywhere they went, Aaron in his black, tailored tuxedo and Joan in her floor-length black gown, they garnered envious looks from everyone they passed. They were an A-list couple and it was apparent to anyone who saw them. At the end of the show, Aaron and Joan took the limousine back to the Bellagio. As they entered it was easy to see that the casino was in full swing. Crowds moved around the slot machines hoping against hope they would be the lucky one to get back more than they had deposited in the one-armed bandits. The table games were also doing a brisk business.

"How about we try our luck at the tables before we turn in?"

"I'll watch you, Aaron. I don't know anything about gambling. All I can see is a bunch of guys laying their chips on the green felt and two seconds later the dealer sweeps all of them into his corner."

"There's a few games where you stand a better chance. Your best odds of winning are at blackjack. Are you familiar with how that's played?"

"That's where you try and get twenty-one points. Right?"

"Yes, but there's a lot more to the game than just being dealt cards and hoping you get dealt a winning hand. You have to keep track in your mind what cards have been played. When it looks like the time is right, you jump in and run up the bet. If you get in when the deck is on a downside you have to realize it and get out quick. The trick is to be playing when the odds are turning in favor of the player. It's complicated but some people are good at it. If they're too good, they call it card counting."

"That's illegal, isn't it?"

"Not illegal but if a casino thinks you're doing it, they can refuse to let you play."

"So, what you're saying is that if they think you stand a chance of beating them, you can't play."

"There, you've got it."

"Not a game I want to play."

"Okay. Well watch me and I'll see if we can win a little."

After a few losing hands, Aaron started winning. He handled his cards like a pro and it was apparent this was not his first trip to a card table at a casino. His pile of chips grew dramatically. "Okay, time to cash in. I can feel it's time for my luck to change. I'm up two grand in just under an hour. Tell you what. Let's go over to the roulette wheel. It has the worst odds of anything in the entire casino. But you can get a big payout if you're lucky. Why don't you pick a color and a number?"

The dealer saw them approach.

"Good evening, madame, sir. Would you like to place a bet?"

Joan asked the obvious question. "What would pay the most if I won it?"

"Double zeroes. It pays thirty-five to one. Would you care to place a bet?"

"I'm game for a try. That's the one I want to bet on. What do you say, Aaron?"

"I've got your back. Let's put the entire two grand on double zero."

Joan was shocked. "Two grand! I didn't know you were going to bet that much. What if I lose?"

"Then we go to our room and you have to try to make me forget about my loss by humoring my every clumsy attempt to 'ravage' you."

"You could do that anyway."

"Just the same, two grand on double zeroes."

"I'll have to ask you to wait for just a moment sir, ma'am, while I clear this with the floor supervisor."

"Certainly."

A very large man in a dark suit came over to the table and looked Aaron and Joan over carefully. He looked as if he had been sent over by Central Casting to play the part of a Mafia hit man. He nodded his head to the dealer indicating the casino would authorize the play. The reality was that the odds of winning and the casino taking the hit were extremely low. In the few moments it took to clear the bet, gawkers began to form a circle around the table to watch such a high stakes bet with such poor odds. After the table accepted the bet, the dealer spun the wheel and seconds later dropped the small ivory ball into it. Joan watched excitedly as the ball spun quickly around the outside of the wheel and as its speed slowed, it fell toward the center of the wheel where it jumped around from colored slot to colored slot. When it came to a stop, the dealer called out immediately. "Double zeroes. We have a winner."

The crowd let out a roar that would have rivaled a touchdown celebration at Notre Dame. They all knew this was a miraculous win. Joan was astounded and couldn't believe she had won. "How much did we win?"

"Thirty-five times two grand. I believe that's about seventy thousand dollars."

"Oh my God. You've made a killing tonight."

"Not me, darling. It's all yours."

"Mine, but I can't take your money."

"Okay, you can give me back my two grand but the rest is yours. The way I look at it I was already a big winner before we ever walked in here. I've just spent one of the most memorable weekends of my life with the most beautiful woman I've ever seen. Now, let's go cash in your chips."

The casino cash window wrote Joan a check for the seventy grand. It was the most money she had ever held at one time in her entire life. "This weekend has been so far beyond anything I've ever experienced. I can't imagine anything grander than this. In Richmond, my life was so far removed from things like this. I could only dream it."

"I'm glad you're having a good time. We will have many more adventures like this. You can count on it."

The evening and then the night passed like a chapter from a romance novel. They would be heading back to Richmond before lunch, so Aaron prompted Joan, "Did you make the call?"

"Which call, darling?"

"The one to your boss back home telling him you wouldn't be coming in to work on Monday or any day from here on out. Aren't you with me on that?"

"If you're sure that's what you want me to do."

"I wouldn't remind you to do it if I weren't sure, would I?"

"I guess not. Okay, I'll call him."

Aaron walked over to Joan and grabbed her from behind with his arms around her waist. She was fixing her hair in the floor-length mirror and looked at his reflection. He squeezed her gently as he stuck his head under her dark blonde hair. "You smell as delicious as you look. You are the most desirable woman I've ever seen. I can't begin to tell you how good you are for me. You make me whole. You've helped me put the past behind me. You are my future, my new beginning. I'm totally happy when you're with me."

"I feel the same. You are the most remarkable man I've ever met."

"Tell you what. I'm going to go downstairs and check out and you try to be ready to go when I get back. I'll alert my pilot that we're on our way to the airport and get the valet to grab us a limo. And if you would, go ahead and make that call to your boss."

"I will. I love you, Aaron."

"And I love you."

Aaron kissed her once more on the back of her neck and walked from the room to take the elevators to make arrangements to leave. Joan went over to the door of the suite and locked it with the deadbolt. She didn't use the phone in the room but instead took her cellphone from her purse. She hit a pre-programmed number.

"Yeah, it's me. Fine. It's all gone exactly the way you wanted it to. He wants me to quit my job and move in with him. You know he's very rich. I might be better off to take him up on his offer instead of yours. I know, I know. I just wanted you to understand that I now have some other options in play. I'm expecting you to do exactly like you promised or I might just take the very generous Aaron Goldman up on his offer. Of course, the last thing I want is another man in my life. At this point, cash is the best companion for me. We'll be home later today. I can expect your envelope to be delivered to my place in the morning? All cash like you said. Yes, I'll do as I said I would."

Joan hung the phone and placed it back in her purse. She had completed the ultimate betrayal to fulfill a previous business arrangement. She didn't need Aaron Goldman or his money. She would have plenty of money of her own in the morning. There would be no strings attached to it. She wouldn't have to pretend to love anyone to get all the things she wanted out of life. Just one more week of convincing Aaron that she loved him and she would be on her way to another life, on her own.

Two nights later, Aaron and Joan lay together in bed back in Richmond. "You remember the Virgin Islands. We talked about it in Vegas. It's somewhere warm. A place where there are palm trees and clear water. Or maybe Cancun or St. Thomas. What do you say?"

Aaron rolled over, withdrawing his spent manhood from her. She moaned as he pulled out. "Oh, baby, I miss it already. Promise you'll fuck me twice a day and I'll go anywhere with you."

"Please, Br'er Rabbit, anywhere but the briar patch."

"What does that mean? Br'er Rabbit. Vicious maybe, but not rabid."

"It's just a line from an Uncle Remus tale. He wrote children's stories about the old South. I forgot; I'm an old man, aren't I?"

"No silly, just mature. Perfectly mature. I love the fact that you're older than me. You know so much about loving a woman that younger men just don't get. You know, like the way you kiss me and rub my body. I'm already climaxing before you're in me. If you're old, I like it."

Joan Williams rolled over on top of Aaron, letting her ample breasts slide along his mouth as she teased him. "When do you want to go?"

"This weekend. Does that work for you?"

"I can hardly wait."

Joan had been staying at Aaron's home the past three days. "A close friend of mine says there's a lot of talk around town about you and me."

"I know. I've heard. Does it bother you?"

"Not if it doesn't upset you."

"Then forget it. You make me happy. That's something I thought would be a long time in coming. Your breasts taste so good. How about I wash you with my tongue?"

"Only if you don't overlook any of those hard to reach places."

"Like this one?"

"Uhmm... That one especially."

Aaron and Joan continued their small talk and lovemaking until late into the night. The unrelenting ringing of the phone by the bed woke him up. The digital clock beside it indicated that it was nine fifteen in the morning.

"Mr. Goldman, this is Victoria."

"Good morning, Victoria. I'm late for work, aren't I?"

"Doesn't mean beans to me. You're the boss. It's peaceful here when you're gone. I get caught up on everything. However, since the members of the board are all starting to arrive, I thought it might be nice for the chairman to be here."

"Shit! I forgot. Keep 'em occupied. I'm on my way."

"What's the rush, darling?"

"Sorry, Joan. I forgot there's a board meeting this morning. Ernest Pearlman will use this to eat me alive if I don't make it. Here, give me a kiss. I'll see you this evening. Listen, take my gold card and go shopping for some things to wear on the trip. When I get back, we'll shove off."

"Bye, handsome. See you tonight."

Aaron literally threw on his clothes and departed. Joan, sat up in the ornate, oversized bed and studied the luxurious surroundings in a way that Alicia never would have thought to do. This sort of lifestyle was completely new to Joan, but one she was quickly growing fond of. She pushed back her hair from her face and dropped down to the floor which was several inches below her feet when sitting on the edge of the bed. Her breasts swung as she walked over to the full length freestanding mirror that Alicia had loved. She stared at herself in the mirror, again pushing back her hair and then running her hands over her still red and burning nipples. She closed her eyes as her movements continued more aggressively and for a moment, she said out loud, "Aaron, you poor, pathetic fool. Today you are in for some surprises."

* * *

Victoria glanced up as Aaron came jogging into the office. "Here, it's the brief you wanted. Better hustle, old man Pearlman is already trying to stir 'em up."

"That bastard. He's continually looking for anything to give himself an edge. Maybe I'll turn the tables on him this morning. Hold my calls... Unless."

"I know, unless it's Miss Williams."

"Great."

When he entered the suite where the board members were already seated around the long oak table, Pearlman stopped in mid-sentence and Aaron just caught his name. "Please continue, Mr. Pearlman. Don't let me being here slow you down at all. I believe in laying all our cards on the table, don't you?"

"I was just saying to the members that as of late you seem a little preoccupied to me. Several times in the last two weeks, my calls to your office have been unanswered. That's just not the way to conduct business in my opinion."

"What is the way you conduct business, Mr. Pearlman? Hiring a private investigator to research the chairman's private life and see if you can find a little dirt somewhere?"

"Well, I..."

"I don't blame you. If I had done that to you and gotten caught, I'd be embarrassed too. That's right. Mr. Pearlman has been paying a private investigator to ask all of my friends and associates personal questions and to research my private life. I can only assume it's so he could find something that would discredit me to the board members and then convince you that the position would be better served if he were the chairman."

Quick to recover and always on the offensive, Pearlman interjected, "I won't deny that I hired a professional to observe your conduct and possibly document that you did not represent our company in a responsible manner."

"And... Go ahead. Be so kind as to share with us the earthshaking revelations that you have discovered about me.

Perhaps you found that I am sharing my home with a wonderful young woman? I'm sure you have. Or how about the earthshattering observation that we eat out several nights a week and even go to the movies once in a while. I wonder did he also discover that since the foundry modernization was completed three months ago, production has already increased over fifty percent and labor costs have dropped by a similar amount. If that holds, and I'm sure it will, profits for the year will go through the roof. I'm sure that things of that nature might be far more interesting to the board, Mr. Pearlman. And I wonder how many other members of the board you've had... Researched?"

This final rhetorical question caused a number of the board members to clear their throats and sit upright in their chairs. That small sentence had been a stroke of genius. He had managed to share the hostility of his rival with the rest of the board members. His coup was complete. Ernest Pearlman went completely silent. Aaron knew better than to consider it "over" though. His enemy was a man who could not be taken lightly. He had won a battle, a significant one, but not the war. This did serve notice to Pearlman that Aaron was also a worthy opponent. He would have to be careful how he went after Aaron Goldman. After all of the theatrics were over, Aaron's presentations to the board went smoothly and any motions he offered to them were rubber-stamped. There was a newfound support for the chairman among the members. Aaron stayed and small-talked with each member and was the last to leave the room. As he passed by Victoria, he handed the same file back to her.

"I've got to tell you, Vicky, that was one of the best moments I've ever experienced."

"Filleted him, huh?"

"Like a smoked salmon. Listen, I'll be out of town 'til next Monday. Just put anything that requires my presence on hold until then."

"She must be quite something, this Miss Williams."

"She is Victoria. She really is."

Aaron basked in the aura of his victory all the way back to Salisbury. He was in a rare mood when he saw Joanie at the door to the bathroom drying her hair. She only had on one of his highly starched dress shirts and she could sense his exuberance the moment she saw him. "What is it?"

"That obvious, huh?"

"You look like the Cheshire cat in 'Alice.' See, I know old children's stories too."

He wrapped his arms around her, her long wet hair drenching him as he kissed her.

"My, whatever you did today, you should do every day."

Aaron began to unbutton the shirt she was wearing. As each button came undone, he pulled that area of the shirt open and kissed the flesh under it. By the time he arrived at the bottom button, Joan was moaning under her breath. Her nipples grew taught and erect and her chest pounded with deep breaths as she stroked his member through his suit pants.

"I need you right now, Joanie, before we go. I want to make love to you every hour this whole weekend. When we leave St. Thomas, I want the hotel maids to remember the couple that messed up every sheet on the island."

"You've sold me. Let's start right now."

"You're on."

"On fire."

Aaron picked her up and carried her to the bed. His life felt whole again. He was in love and Alicia was finally behind him.

They made love with an intensity that he had not felt since his youth. When they were done, he lay beside her, their limbs entwined, unable to remove each other from their touch. After an hour, Aaron heard the doorbell ringing down the hall. "I think there's someone at the door."

"It's almost 9 p.m. Were you expecting someone tonight?"

"No, our flight leaves at 7 a.m. The last thing I want tonight is company. I would prefer to just lie here with you. That hour went by pretty fast."

The bell rang again. Aaron threw on a bathrobe and Joan put his suit coat on and followed behind him, curious who would be there so late. At the door he found a familiar but quite unexpected visitor, one he had not seen for several months. "Freda, what are you doing here?"

Detective Payne stepped into the foyer. She could not help but notice the young woman in her hastily thrown-on attire. "I'm sorry, I should have called first. I just wanted to tell you, in person."

"Tell me what?"

"Your wife has been found."

"My God. Is she... Alive?"

"Yes, she was the victim of a shooting, but she is expected to recover. She's in Louisiana."

"This is unbelievable! After all this time. I'm stunned."

There was a look of concern on Joan's face as she came over to Aaron and put her arms around him, in front of the detective.

He was speechless for a moment.

Freda continued, "The Louisiana State Police have been informed of the search up here and they have posted a watch over her at the hospital. I'm going to go down there with Bob McDermott in the morning. We thought you might like to go with us."

"Yes, of course I would. What time are you leaving?"

"We'll pick you up on the way. Plane leaves at 10 a.m. So you'll need to call ahead for a ticket and be ready about eight. United flight 1240."

"I'll be ready. And Freda?"

"Yes?"

"Did they say how she was, or how she got there?"

"I'd rather you see her for yourself. We all need to talk with the authorities there before we jump to any conclusions. From what I understand, she has some problems, but she is alive."

Aaron detected obvious disappointment in her voice. She apparently didn't know that he had started seeing Joan.

"I just wanted... Well, to tell you. Anyway, I'll see you in the morning."

"Thank you, Freda. I appreciate your coming out this late to tell me the news."

"No problem. Goodnight."

Aaron turned to see tears in Joan's eyes. As long as he had waited to hear that Alicia was alive, he now realized how complicated this was all becoming.

"Aaron. I do love you. I really do. You know that. But..."

"What, Joan? But what?"

"I'm going to get my stuff together and go back to my place. Under this set of circumstances, I think that's what I need to do. If, if you decide later that we should be together, then maybe it will work out. You're still married, Aaron. You have to take care of your wife first. Then we can think about us, if that's what you want."

"I love you, Joan. I've been straight with you. I thought my wife was dead. It's been so long. I couldn't have known."

"It's okay, Aaron. You take care of her first. I'm all right."

Joan turned and went back to the bedroom. This was, of course, the perfect out for Joan. Her leaving was as much Aaron's idea as hers. She had earned her pound of flesh.

12

"Nice to meet you, Mr. Goldman. I'm Captain Wheeler with the Louisiana State Police. Before we take you to see your wife, we need to talk. Let's sit down for a minute. The administrator is letting us use an office and we can get you a coffee if you want one. Want me to have one brought in for you?"

"That's not necessary. I'm anxious to see my wife."

"I understand, but please sit down."

"I've got to tell you, Captain, you're making me pretty damned nervous. What's the problem with Alicia? Is she in a coma, paralyzed, or what?"

"'Or what' is pretty close, Mr. Goldman. From the pictures that I have been given by Detective Payne of your wife before her disappearance, you probably won't recognize her. The only way we found out her identity was from an old set of fingerprints they had in the national database. We print any shooting victim as a routine procedure and luckily, they matched."

"How... How is she different?"

"I'm sure you've already prepared yourself for the worst, so just consider this better than never finding her or finding her dead."

"I'm a grown man, for Christ's sake, tell me what's the problem?"

"First, Mrs. Goldman has a major drug problem. She is heavily addicted to heroin. A severe case. It's to the point that she probably doesn't have a strong vein left in her body to shoot up with."

"You've got to be joking! She's a health fanatic."

"A lot of people, especially young women being kidnapped for the prostitution racket are involuntarily hooked on heroin."

"Prostitution racket! What the hell are you talking about here? You couldn't have beaten Alicia into doing anything like that. She'd die first."

"That's not too far removed a description of what happened. The old Mrs. Goldman, was, in effect, killed, by dope and physical abuse. Doesn't take that long for them to be willing to do just about anything to get a fix. That's more than likely how this happened. The doctor tells me it's to the point that it has diminished her mental faculties as well. From interviews with the help at the bar where she was shot, we do know that she was doing tricks for the owner. He's a small-time pimp with a long rap sheet for prostitution and fencing stolen goods. We're pretty sure that he wasn't involved with the kidnapping but he is a good lead to whoever that is. The shooting is a still a puzzle. It appeared to everyone there that there was no purpose to it. The guy who did it was either a nut-case, or he may have been somehow connected to the person who took your wife. Could be that the abductor started to worry that she might lead back to him and paid somebody to get rid of her. For my money, that's the most reasonable scenario."

Aaron's words were slow and studied. "Alicia was working as a whore. Is that what you're telling me? My wife was out fucking any grease ball truck driver for fifty dollars?"

"I don't know about all the small details, but she was definitely working as a prostitute. I know that's hard for you to accept but, believe me, Mr. Goldman, hundreds of women a year, from all kinds of backgrounds are kidnapped and forced into prostitution.

Hell, a number are carried to the Far East and sold into carnal slavery. It does happen, a lot more than you or anyone not aware of the problem might believe."

"I gotta tell you, Captain, that's pretty hard to believe. My wife was a very strong, straight-minded woman. That just doesn't seem possible. You mentioned her appearance. Other than the heroin problem, how is it that I wouldn't recognize her?"

"To be honest with you, she doesn't even resemble the pictures we were sent. She looks twenty years older and even her features are different. I'm not trying to depress you, but you should be prepared for it when you see her. The doctor says that her long-term prognosis is not good for several reasons. Chronic addicts have an extremely high recidivism rate. They're not cured very often. The more serious problem facing her is that she is HIV positive."

"Good Lord. She has AIDS?"

"I'm sorry. Could have been contracted from a shared needle, sex, any number of ways from the environment she's been in."

"I don't understand. If she was left to work at a bar, why didn't she just call somebody to help her? We could have gotten her home anytime, if she had just called."

"You are obviously not aware of the pull heroin has on the mind. Unless she thought you would have kept furnishing her drugs, she would have no interest in you, or anyone for that matter. That's about the worst of it, Mr. Goldman. We have a full-blown investigation under way into the shooting and also into finding her abductor if he's still around. Are you up to seeing her now?"

"As much as I'm going to be."

Aaron entered the private room and walked over to the foot of the bed. Alicia was hooked up to any number of tubes and monitors. The rhythmic click of the heart monitor by the bed indicated a steady heartbeat. As she lay there asleep, he looked closely at her face. The look on his own face was as revealing as the changes to hers. He forced himself to address her. "I'm here, Alicia. It's Aaron. What has happened to you, baby? Who did this to you?"

He stood over her for almost ten minutes, just looking at this stranger his wife had become. As he stared at her, her eyes blinked several times and then opened. The fire from deep inside them that had always been a clear indicator of her boundless spirit was gone. They were a dull gray. She looked up at Aaron, with apparently no recognition of her husband. "Are you a doctor?"

"No, I'm Aaron."

"Man, have you got any shit on you? I'm hurting pretty bad. Can you help me out?"

Aaron held back tears at the realization of what a pathetic creature this was lying before him.

"What did you say your name was? Abraham? Don't you hear me asking for some shit, man? Where the hell are we? Oh, the hospital still. Hey, Abraham, how about getting the doctor for me?"

"I'll do that."

He turned and left the room. He could deal with no more for the moment. He would settle his nerves and try to rekindle some memory in her later.

* * *

After another week, Alicia's wounds were sufficiently healed so that she could be released. She was still very much dependent on heroin and only semi-coherent. Her long-term memory was nonexistent and she still had not recognized Aaron. He made arrangements to have her transferred back to Richmond, into the

Dogwood Center, a private clinic for wealthy alcoholics and drug addicts. He spent a small amount of time at the center almost daily, carefully watching for signs of improvement. On this particular morning, he was greeted with a surprise as he entered the lobby. There, standing at the reception desk was Alicia's estranged sister.

"What are you here for, Delores? To claim your final superiority over her now that she's been reduced to the level of a second grader?"

"There's no reason for you to try and hurt me, Aaron. Disagreements or not, she's still my sister and I don't want to see her suffering. I just wanted to see if maybe I could be of help, maybe some childhood memories might bring her around. Do you object to my seeing her?"

"I can't see where it makes any difference. She still doesn't know who I am, so I doubt seriously if she'll know who you are. Who knows, you may get along better like this."

Delores entered the room and walked over to Alicia's bedside. "Hey, Alicia, how's my baby sister?" Even though she was startled by her appearance, she remained calm, stroking her forehead. "Do you know who I am?"

"You're not Mary Lou, are you?"

"No dear, I'm Delores. Who is Mary Lou?"

"I love Mary Lou. We love each other. Where is she?"

"I'm sorry, I don't know her. I'll try and find her for you. Is that okay?"

She nodded affirmatively.

"Alicia, I know we have had problems getting along over the years, but I want you to know that I'm here for you. I'm going to stay with you. If you need anything, you just ask me. Do you understand?"

"I need a hit. Can you help me? The doctor here is a piece of shit. He don't want to give me a hit. Doctor K was mean, but at least he would take care of me. He gave me a fix anytime. Whenever I was hurting."

"Who is Doctor K?"

"You don't want to know him. He'll lock you up and make you stay there. Don't talk to him."

"He might give me a fix for you. Do you know how I can get in touch with him?"

"Ask Danny; he'll know. He knows him too. Get me some shit, will you? Please?"

"I'll get the doctor, baby. Just try and be still."

* * *

Thurman Roe had only been back to his apartment a few minutes after a late night session at the Henrico County Sheriff's Department communications center. The loud ringing of his phone brought him out of the shower, still dripping wet, his hair laced with shampoo. "I hope this is important. I haven't had one uninterrupted hour in a month. What's up?"

"Hey T, the hot line just went off. I got a squad car on the way to the phone booth already. It's the Goldman line."

"No shit! Can you put me through to the squad car?"

"Hold on."

Thurman could hear the call being placed over the police channel in the background. In seconds he was in touch with the officer riding shotgun in the squad car.

"Yeah, Thurman, we're about three blocks out. You want us to go ahead and collar whoever's on the phone?"

"No. Just keep the suspect in sight. Don't lose him. I'll be there in fifteen minutes. I want you to tail the suspect 'til I get there."

"You got it."

Thurman threw his clothes back on and, disheveled as he was, ran to his car and squealed out of his apartment project's driveway, headed toward the payphone he had supervised the surveillance on with no results for so many months. In his typical analytical fashion he tried to formulate a reason in his mind why anyone would be calling Goldman this long after the abduction. The chance of a legitimate late-night call by a friend or business associate from this particular phone, situated in a high crime, low rent commercial district would be extremely remote. It had to be tied to the case. Even a wrong number from this particular payphone to the Goldman number would be pretty hard to believe, with over two hundred thousand numbers in the area. He spotted the black and white a block from the phone and pulled in behind it.

"Okay guys, I'm here. Where's the caller?"

"Well, there's no way to be sure it's the same person that called Goldman a few minutes earlier, but the guy who was using it when we pulled in went into the video porn shop two doors past the phone. You want us to pick him up for questioning?"

"Probably so, but first, here's what I want to do. Give me a couple of minutes. I want to go in behind him and see what the guy is up to. What's he look like?"

"Short, male, Caucasian. Maybe forty, forty-five with glasses... And bald. Wearing a dark overcoat, kind of shabby looking. If he comes out, we'll pick him up. You got five minutes from right now and then we're coming in behind you. And Thurman..."

"Yeah?"

"Don't approach the suspect. Something goes wrong it's our ass. Understand?"

"No problem. I'm no hero. Here goes."

Thurman entered the porno shop and tried to blend in with the seedy looking characters that frequented the place. Toward the back of the store, he noticed the suspect the officers had described. He was handing a bill to the clerk, apparently to get change to use in one of the XXX-rated video machines in the rear of the store. Each machine was in a small cubicle by itself. Privacy was essential to the viewers of these videos as the great majority masturbated into a sock or prophylactic while they watched the seedy videos. He stayed back as the suspect entered the cubicle.

He couldn't help but feel that he recognized the man but he needed to get a closer look. He eased to the back of the store. The cubicle door the suspect had entered was swinging open and it became apparent that he had left through another door just beyond it. Thurman slipped through that door also. It led down a narrow, debris-strewn hallway with seven or eight doors closed tightly along the way. As he passed each, the unmistakable sounds of prostitutes cajoling their johns could be heard.

A door near the end of the hall closed just ahead of him. That had to be his man. Thurman felt his shoulder harness to be sure that his thirty-eight special was properly mounted for retrieval if needed. Satisfied that his piece was in order, he slowly pushed open the door and entered the room. The lights were off and the air was quite ripe with the smell of sweat and too many nights of unwashed sheets. He stared hard into the darkened room. Finally, he became aware that the bed on the far end was occupied. Not knowing exactly what the best course of action would be, Thurman brazenly spoke up in his firmest authoritative voice, "Police! Listen up! Cut the lights on."

It sounded stupid to him, even as he said it. He now wished he had waited for the officers before entering the room. He knew only too well he was a technician, not a streetwise officer. There was only a gurgling sound coming from the bed. He slowly approached, withdrawing his pistol as he walked. As he got to the edge of the bed, he could just barely see a dark haired woman slowly moving her head incoherently as droplets of blood ran from her eyes and nose and from the piano wire that had been drawn and tied around her neck so tightly that no air or circulation could possibly pass through her windpipe.

"Pretty nasty, huh, son?"

Thurman was so startled that he dropped his revolver and was rendered momentarily speechless. He regained his composure quickly. "You... What are you doing here?"

"I just came by to see you, Thurman. Here, I brought you some evidence from a very recent crime."

"What crime?"

In one graceful sweep, the man's arm, with a razor sharp blade protruding from his outstretched hand, sliced Thurman's face almost in two. He groaned, and moved his hands to his bloodied face.

"Why, your murder, son."

The blade struck again, this time to his mid-section. He now dropped his hands to his stomach; his face carrying a look of absolute terror coupled with disbelief. His normally symmetrical face appeared to be a Picasso with its main features redesigned by the razor wielding artist. He dropped to his knees then slid forward, his head stopping his body's forward movement toward the floor. A quickly growing, dark circle of his bodily fluids filled the space around him. His attacker calmly turned and exited the room. Noticing two officers approaching the front door he stepped into one of the curtained video screening cubes and as they passed he stepped out behind them. They entered the room with guns drawn only to see Thurman lying in the dark red pool of blood.

His murderer stepped out onto the street and disappeared into the crowded city. As he walked off unnoticed, sirens blared from the street and slid to a stop in front of the shop of horror.

Allowing Thurman to enter alone, even though it was his operation, had been an error in judgment they should never have let occur. By their own account, it was one of the bloodiest and most troubling discoveries of either officer's long career on the force. It was apparent that Thurman had been completely gutted.

13

Rick Sheay had just opened a beer and sat down in front of the TV in his dingy walkup apartment. He put the fresh can down on the table top after pushing the dozen or so empties out of the way to make room. Having no friends, a knock on the door could only mean one person.

"Open up, Rick! It's me. I need to talk with you."

"It ain't locked, just push. The fuckin' hinge is busted."

His assumption proved correct as a long-time associate made his way into the room. "Welcome to the palace. You got somebody else you want me to hit for you?"

"You screwed up, Rick."

"Like hell, you say! I shot two whores. And you only paid me for the one."

"And the one I paid you for is not dead."

"That ain't possible. I pumped two shots in her fuckin' chest. She's dead. I guarantee it."

"Actually, you did far more than guarantee it, Rick, you bet your life on it."

"Come on now. Quit fuckin' with me, Kale. She's dead, ain't she?"

"I don't fuck with people, Rick, and no, she's quite alive. Now Rick, put both of your hands on the table in front you."

Rick remained in his chair, not readily responding to his guest's demands. In only seconds, a pistol was produced from under Kale's jacket. Rick then moved his hands, palms down onto the small table in front of him, knocking over the assortment of beer cans as he did.

"That a boy. Now, I want you take this pen and piece of paper and write what I tell you."

"You're crazy! What the fuck do you want from me?"

"If you don't want your brains on the table in three seconds, Rick, you'll start writing."

"All right, be careful with that thing. I'm writing already; I'm writing. Just tell me what you want."

"That's better. I did so want us to remain friends 'til the end."

* * *

Not a moment had passed since the shooting at the Gandy Dancer that Danny didn't jump at every unexpected noise. He understood fully the implications of the murder of Mary Lou and the attempt on Agnes' life. Kale had helped him make a lot of money over the last few years but he was a very disturbed and dangerous individual. To make money in the prostitution business you had to be willing to deal with many unsavory personalities. There was always risk to these joint ventures. He sensed that Kale was far worse than most. Realizing he was the link to him made Danny a liability that Kale would never accept. He was a marked man and he knew it. The cops knew the sort of rackets Danny was involved in but they never considered him a suspect. He never mentioned Kale to them as the whores all came from twisted backgrounds and Agnes had undoubtedly had her share of undesirables in her past. At this moment, Danny had no way of knowing the firestorm he was in the middle due to Agnes having her fingerprints traced. Kale knew only too well. Any tracks would have to be removed.

Danny got home very late. Between cleaning up the Gandy Dancer, assuring his other whores that they were not going to be gunned down, and talking with a steady stream of investigators, he was exhausted. He walked over to every window, checking the locks and making certain the shades were drawn completely tight. Satisfied that all was in order he went the liquor cabinet and poured himself a shot of straight whiskey. Without the assistance of alcohol, he'd never be able to fall asleep. He sat in the overstuffed recliner that faced the front door of his small framed home. He wished there were more lights on the street out front but city workers didn't like to work in this part of town and only an order from the city big-wheels could make them replace blown out light fixtures. That order seldom came and the street stayed immersed in darkness most of the time. Danny turned on the television only to see a reporter discussing the shooting. That was the last thing he wanted to see so he quickly switched to the weather channel, totally uninterested in the report but needing some background distraction to settle his nerves. After two more shots of whiskey, he finally fell into a deep sleep in the chair.

Danny's sleep was fitful at best. Slowly he began to stir as he felt what was unmistakably a bug of sorts crawling up his arm. Dazed, he swatted at it with his eyes still closed. The second swing was more toward his upper arm and by the time he was awake enough to realize this was not a dream, the intruder had apparently stung him on the neck. He quickly came to full consciousness and reached to the spot where the pain had been generated. At that moment, a small table lamp beside the chair came on with no help from Danny. He knew he was no longer alone and he didn't need to guess who had joined him.

"Good evening, Danny, my friend."

Kale sat on the couch beside Danny's chair. He had a revolver in his hand.

"Kale, I never told them a thing. They questioned me for hours and I told them I didn't have any idea who would have shot the whores. You're safe with me."

"I know, Danny. I know. But you see, Danny. These question and answer sessions with the authorities never really end. They keep coming back, over and over, and after a while you forget what you told them last week or maybe last month. That's the problem with lying, Danny. You have to tell another lie to cover the previous. After a while, you can't remember what you said at all. It never pays to lie."

"I haven't changed my story at all. I know exactly what I told them and I won't ever change my story. Umm... My head is starting to swirl, I'm getting dizzy. Too much whiskey. I need some water. You mind if I get a drink?"

"Not at all, Danny. But, my friend, you don't need water. That's not your problem."

"What... What's... My... Problem?" Danny asked, his voice breaking between each word.

"Drugs, Danny. Drugs. You have just overdosed on heroin. Really pure heroin. But I can help you. I have another needle right here with me that can counteract the effects and save you Danny."

"I need it. I'm starting to get too dizzy to think straight."

"I know, I know. But first, a couple of questions and I need straight answers. No lying here."

"The truth, Kale. You'll get only the truth. What do you want to know?"

"You never mentioned my name to anyone during any of the questioning?"

"Never, not once. Swear on my mother's grave."

"No need to swear, Danny. I believe you. Now, one more question."

"Anything. Quickly please. I'm starting to pass out."

"Did anyone ever ask you how Agnes came to your place?"

"Sure, they asked all kinds of questions but I never told them nothing."

"Danny, you mean to tell me they accepted nothing as an answer to a question about a murder?"

"Well, I mean I gave them some bullshit answers but never mentioned you in any way. I swear. Please, the medicine."

"That's really unfortunate, Danny. You don't remember what you told them exactly but you do remember exactly that you never mentioned me."

"That's right, one hundred percent."

"Okay, my friend, I'm satisfied. Here, let me give you another shot and relieve you of the effects of the heroin."

Doctor K gave a small squirt on the syringe plunger to make certain the drug was at the top and then expertly gave Danny another shot, this time in the forearm. Almost immediately, Danny became very quiet, his eyes rolling up to the tops of their lids. His body shuddered once, twice, and then finally a short but powerful twinge and his head fell forward. Doctor K took the syringe, unconcerned with fingerprints as he was wearing surgical gloves for that express purpose, and clasped Danny's fingers around it tightly before dropping it to the floor.

"Poor Danny, unable to live with the shame of turning sweet young girls into whores, you wound up killing yourself with drugs. Your parents will be so proud."

Doctor K exited quietly out of the back door, locking it as he left.

* * *

Virginia Industrial was braced for a power struggle, unequaled in its long, storied history. Sides had been drawn with board members backing either Aaron Goldman or Ernest Pearlman. This morning's meeting was the culmination of that struggle for control. A new factor for Aaron to deal with had been the revelation that his sister-in-law had acquired a huge block of common stock in the company over the past few months. It had been accomplished quietly and most effectively. Angus McVeigh had earned his pound of flesh, as promised. Delores had enough votes to swing a proxy vote in whatever direction she wished. Aaron was treading in dangerous water.

"Fellow board members, I want you all to understand that I have no personal animus toward Aaron Goldman. I am interested only in the long-term security of my investment in this company. All of you have the same interest, I'm sure. The respect that the business leaders of this community, meaning regulators and the banks, have in our management determines our success or failure. It's that simple. So, my question to you all is do we trust the future to a man whose wife, the daughter of Carl Thompson, is confined to a nursing home as a result of a vicious kidnapping, while he is living, that's right, living, with a woman many years his junior?

"To me, and I'm sure to a lot of you, as well as the business community at large, this is a serious breach of ethics. This indicates to me a lack of stability and casts doubt over his ability to make the tough decisions and more importantly, to do the right thing even when it's difficult. I have with me this morning a copy of an order placed by Victoria Cousineau, Mr. Goldman's personal assistant, whom I'm sure most of you know, for two tickets to Cancun. Victoria is on our payroll, I might add. I don't get her to book any personal vacations for my family and I'm certain that none of you do either. These tickets were for a pricey vacation that Aaron Goldman and his new lady friend, Joan Williams, were leaving on the morning after Alicia Goldman arrived, critically wounded at a hospital in Louisiana. The Goldmans are, of course, still married and apparently our Chairman had given up his own efforts to find her even though the police and every other responsible agency had not.

"I was outraged when I heard of this. Even worse, Mr. Goldman commandeered the company's jet and used it to whisk his new lady friend to Las Vegas for a gala weekend at our expense. It's time for a change here and I hope that you will agree with me and let's get this company headed back in the right direction."

There were some distinctively different looks on the faces of the directors after this speech by Ernest Pearlman. Aaron quickly glanced toward Delores to see her response. She held enough voting power now to move the company away from him in favor of Pearlman if she desired. Like a consummate poker player, she remained expressionless. She was far too smart to make her thoughts known prior to exacting favors from whichever side she finally took. She would wait for the right moment and then make her wishes known, in far more private surroundings than these.

Flushed, Aaron took his turn. "Thank you for your thoughts, Mr. Pearlman. As distasteful as I find your comments concerning my private life, I have no intention of defending how I spend my time away from the office. It plays no part in my decisions here and I also assure you all that I have not overlooked my obligations to my wife. She has been in a private care facility for quite some time and it's doubtful that she will ever be a functional member of society again. She is getting the best of care and will continue to as long as she's alive. Her ability to be a wife, however, is gone. This has been a personal tragedy for me as we had a wonderful relationship. Life goes on and things change whether we want them to or not. That's the position I found myself in and I have done nothing to discredit this company or myself.

"As Fred Burns will show you later this evening, our sales are continuing to grow. We've taken the company through an extensive modernization period and maintained profits during the course of these improvements. Unless you have personally been in a situation such as I found myself after Alicia's abduction, you would probably have a very difficult time understanding what I have been through.

"Many of you have privately given me your support and I am forever grateful for that. However, the question you now have to ask yourself is, have I been a good custodian of your investment in Virginia Industrial? Not whether or not you approve of who I choose to spend my own time with. Have I made you money? Has there been any doubt that your interests and mine in this company are the same? Those are solid growth and good returns with a stable outlook for the future. I think you all know what the answers are to these questions. Your faith in me as your Chairman will ensure that this positive direction is continued, Mr. Pearlman's views to the contrary.

"As far as having Victoria Cousineau arrange for my vacations, she merely places a call to a travel agency who actually does the work. Her handling these small details allows me to focus on the things that you pay me to do and the differences in what you have to pay us dictates that she handle these matters.

"As far as the use of the company plane, I immediately wrote a check to the company for the cost of using the plane. As Chairman, I have the option to use the plane for personal flights as long as I pay the costs associated with that use. So, Mr.

Pearlman's accusations are groundless and their intent should be obvious to everyone in this room. I hope none of you ever finds yourself in the personal hell that I found myself. I've done what I had to do to keep my sanity. In spite of all my problems, I always put the company ahead of myself and the P&L statements show that I'm correct. That's really all I have to say. Thank you. Let's take a short break and then Mr. Burns will go over the quarterly figures."

While the members took the opportunity to grab a drink and stretch their legs, Aaron walked to his office down the darkened corridor. He sat down in his chair in the quiet room, still upset with the personal attacks on his character. He was startled by Ernest Pearlman's entrance right behind him. Pearlman brazenly walked over to the front of Aaron's desk, lit his cigar, which he knew Aaron detested, and continued his berating.

"Your remarks were convincing, Goldman. If I didn't know you better, I might be convinced, myself."

"What do you want from me?"

"Out. I want you out of this company. I'm willing to offer a premium for your stock to have you and whatever youngster you wish to sleep with, head down a separate road."

"My private life is none of your concern."

"When it affects my pocketbook, it is. And, I have to tell you…"

"Tell me what?"

"I'm not an idiot. You married the Thompson girl to get exactly where you are today. I never believed your charade for a minute. Now you have it all, the company, an incompetent wife, and a young mistress. The best of everything, right Goldman?"

"Just get out of my office, Pearlman. You disgust me. Just because your own thoughts are so perverted, don't give me credit for them. Now get out of here. Anything you have to say to me will have to be at a board meeting. Do I need to call security?"

"I'm going. But let me tell you something, since you're so confident of your position. You're heading for a real fall. I'm not an easy man to get rid of. I've got you all figured out. Don't rest too comfortably. You're in for a real surprise."

"More threats? That seems to be your forte."

"Thank you for your time, Mr. Goldman. I'll be in the board room with the directors. No need to call security. I'm not what you need to be concerned about. By the way, I find your sister-in-law a particularly delightful woman. We seemed to... well, hit it off, almost from the start."

* * *

Delores had been staying with Alicia for weeks. She would arrive early each morning, and remain until after dinner. Alicia's condition, her dependency and vulnerability had pulled her sister back to her side. For many years, Delores had felt an outcast in her own family. This was as much a time for healing for her as it was Alicia. She had arrived far later than usual today as the board meeting had kept her occupied for most of the morning. She was startled when Aaron entered the room, just moments after her.

"Aaron, what are you doing here this late? You don't usually show up after visiting hours."

"Things are not going well for me right now. You saw I got pretty beat up at the board meeting today. I thought seeing Alicia might help. When I see her sleeping like this, I sometimes think back to how it used to be and wonder why all of this happened to her, to us. It took what we had, and I guess I just miss it. Look, her hair is turning dark again at the roots. I hate that white color."

"Yes, I'm going to have my personal hairstylist come over tomorrow and change it back to its original color. Now that the roots are coming out, she can match the color closely. She does look very peaceful lying there. God only knows what she has been through. I'm not sure I even want to hear the details."

"Delores, I do want to thank you, for being here with her so much. I really believe it's helping her. What do you think? Is she getting better?"

"It's slow. Sometimes I think she'll be this way forever. Then, once in a while, she'll ask me something that makes me think she's remembering. You know, yesterday morning she asked if I had ever gone with her to a circus. She kept talking about an elephant. When we were kids, we went to the circus every year... She always loved the elephants. I keep thinking that one morning she'll wake up and be her old self. Whether she does or not, I'm gonna be here for her. And Aaron..."

"What Delores?"

"What would you say to me taking responsibility for her? I know that you thought you'd never see her again and well...you quite naturally found someone else. I understand that. No one wants to be alone. You did all you could. It would make it easier on you. You could get on with your life. I would petition the court to name me her legal guardian. I'll be completely responsible for her care. You could still come see her whenever you wanted. You'll always be welcome. It's something I want to do. After all the years going for each other's throat, I want my sister back. I realize now how important my family is. My parents are gone, but she's still here and needs me. I want to do this. She'd be better off living with me, away from this sort of environment. I'll keep a nurse for her as long as it's needed. She'll get the best of care."

"I don't doubt that for a moment, Delores. Tell you what. Let me think on it for a while and I'll get back with you."

"Do you have some reservations about her being with me, because I'm a lesbian? My friends? My lifestyle? I'm not nearly as off center as you might imagine. And, to tell you the truth…"

"The truth about what?"

"I don't want to shock you, but Alicia had been having a relationship with a woman."

"Not Alicia. No way!"

"Trust me. I'm sure of it. If you would talk to the Louisiana State Police that found her, you'll find that she was involved with the woman that was killed. Her name was Mary Lou."

"The black woman?"

"Yes."

"I don't know where that came from…but I don't believe it for a minute."

"You find it shocking or humiliating to think that your wife was sleeping with a woman?"

"Neither, I just don't believe it. She was too set against that to ever fall into that sort of behavior."

"I won't argue the morality of homosexuality with you, Aaron, but what I've told you is the truth. That's neither here nor there now, though. It would be better for you, her, and me too, if I became her guardian. The court will grant you a divorce without taking the position that you were abandoning her. You could remarry if you wanted."

"I hear you, Delores. Just let me think it over."

"Please give it serious consideration, Aaron. I've thought about it a lot and I'm determined to do this. I would certainly remember your cooperation at the company board meetings. From the way things seemed to be going for you today, you need all the support you can get."

Aaron could not help but feel a deliberate power play was under way by Alicia's remark. "If I give you what you're asking for here, what about Alicia's claim on any company stock? I suppose you'd feel that she would take her half of the company with her and you'd want to exercise those votes also. Right?"

"Half? Alicia and my family controlled all of the stock before you married her. I'd bet a tidy sum that a good lawyer could persuade the courts to let her keep all the stock and give you a buy-out based on an alimony type relationship. And, I have very good attorneys. Look, Aaron. You're in kind of a tough spot here. I'm not out to ruin you personally. In fact, I'd like to see you happy and getting on with your life. There's no need for a pissing contest between us.

"I've got a feeling, just a feeling mind you, that Ernest Pearlman is heading for a lot of personal problems that are going to take his attention away from Virginia Industrial. You, with my support and Alicia's stock being carefully voted by her big sister, in her own best interest, could pretty well have the company back under a close, almost entirely 'family,' control. Who knows? We might wind up buying back all of the outstanding stock and become entirely private again. Anyway, you just think about it, Aaron. I'm very amenable to a working relationship with you. Of course, your pit bull would have to go."

"You mean, Burns? Fred?"

"Who else? You probably don't see that side of him, what with him kissing your proverbial ass around the clock, but he is not the kind of person I like having involved in my financial affairs. He tends to suck power and money from anyone around him and I like to pick my own charities. You understand, don't you?"

"I see. Give me some time and I'll get back with you. This is a lot to digest all at one time. I do appreciate your concern for Alicia. I wanted you to know that."

"I know. Thanks."

14

Delores checked the brass mailbox next to the door of her stately brownstone. Rain was beginning to fall and the dark night was routinely being punctuated by strong bursts of lightning. A far darker storm cloud was approaching. Somewhat surprised to find the box empty, she unlocked the door and entered. It had been a very long day. She was exceedingly satisfied with her power play at the nursing home. The look of helplessness on Aaron's face had greatly enriched her own feeling of wellbeing and satisfaction. Only seconds after removing her coat and shoes, pouring a shot of brandy and collapsing onto her overstuffed chair, someone was beating on her door. She thought, *"Must be Diane. She's pissed that I haven't been seeing her. I'm just too tired for company tonight."*

She walked to the intercom beside the door. Even in her well secured neighborhood, it paid to be prudent when letting people in. "Hello. Who is it?"

"Miss Thompson, I need to speak with you a moment about Aaron Goldman. I won't keep you long. It's pouring out here. Could you spare me just a moment?"

Delores cracked the door and peered out of the gap left by the door chain. Her visitor was short, balding, and looked harmless. "Just for a moment. I've had a long day."

Delores opened the door and the rain-soaked visitor meekly entered.

"Here, give me your coat. You're drenched."

"Thank you, Miss Thompson. I appreciate you're allowing me a minute of your time. Staying at the clinic with your sister all day has to be draining."

"How do you know that? Do you work for Aaron?"

"No. In fact, I'm a private investigator and I work for a Mr. Ernest Pearlman. Are you familiar with him?"

"I know the name. He's got something to do with Virginia Industrial, doesn't he?"

"I admire your gift for understatement, Miss Thompson. You might say that Mr. Pearlman... He's a large stockholder, as you know, who is quite disenchanted with your brother-in-law."

"And, you must be out looking for dirt on him. Am I right?"

"Just the truth. I'm paid to find out what the facts are. May I sit down? I've had a long drive today and I'm beat. Left Louisiana this morning and I've been fighting rain pretty much all day."

"Louisiana? I assume you've been down there checking on what happened to my sister?"

"That's correct. By the way, how is she? I've never actually met her, though I have seen pictures of her. A startling change."

"She's somewhat better. I have great hopes for her. Now, what can I help you with? I'm not that familiar with Aaron or his business dealings. The company belonged to my father and he didn't approve of me. He left the business to Alicia and Aaron when he died."

"That's not quite true, Delores. May I call you Delores?"

"It's probably best that we keep this on a business level. Miss Thompson would be better. Now, what do you mean, that's not quite true?

"As I understand the listings at the SEC, he left the business to Alicia. All of the stock. Technically, the lion's share of the stock is still in her name. Though large blocks of shares have recently been purchased by an equity account managed by Angus McVeigh. I assume he's acting on your behalf. That actually is obvious enough, you know."

"I see you're very thorough."

"Bear with me a minute, Miss Thompson. I have something I want you to listen to. My coat?"

"By the door. On the hanger."

He retrieved a small recorder from the coat pocket and set it on the coffee table between them. Delores, more than a little taken aback by the man's assessment of the company's stock situation, tried to remain calm and in possession of her poker face.

"The sound is a little scratchy, but I'm pretty sure you'll be able to make it out."

"What is this?"

"Just listen; it's self-explanatory."

From the recorder, the voices of Aaron Goldman and Fred Burns were easily recognizable. It was obviously a phone conversation.

"You tapped their line?"

"About thirty minutes ago. Quiet. Just listen!"

"Fred, I just finished talking with Delores. She was at the clinic. The bitch is practically living there. She wants to become Alicia's guardian, to ask the fucking court for legal custody!"

"You can't let that happen. She gets custody, she takes over Alicia's legal affairs, and she controls the largest block of votes in Virginia Industrial. You told her no, didn't you?"

"I didn't want to seem overly concerned. I just put her off to buy some time. Let me tell you, she's a headstrong, butch dyke and she seems to be dead set on doing this."

"You think she's trying to gain control of the company by getting custody of Alicia?"

"Think? Do I think she is? Fred, aren't you listening? What else would she want? You think she's on a guilt trip for being at odds with her family for most of her life? She just wants what everybody wants... Money. Mine and yours. As a matter of fact, she mentioned you by name. She doesn't like you for shit. What do you think we should do?"

"No matter what, she can't be appointed guardian."

"Delores even said that Alicia is starting to remember things. This could all start to come apart. I should never have listened to you. You said your man was a pro, that this would never happen. Now this could all blow up in our faces. Why didn't he just kill her and get it over with?"

"You would eventually have become the prime suspect under any other circumstances. This way, you are the loving husband who stood by your poor wife through it all. You would still be the heartbroken spouse if you hadn't started living with that bimbo. I told you not to do it. You could have just fucked her and been done with it. It's not like there aren't millions of women out there looking for a rich boyfriend. You might as well put a sign on your forehead that reads 'suspect.' There's no alternative now. Alicia's got to be eliminated. No wife, no battle for custody, and you get control of her stock. End of story."

"I don't know, Fred. This is all getting too complicated. There's too many people watching. Hell, her sister is with her all day, pretending to be so concerned about her baby sister. Fuck. It turns my stomach to see that bitch there."

"I'm thinking that you should tell Delores to go ahead and take Alicia home. That way if there were an accident, Delores, who stands to inherit nothing from her, would be the negligent party. And if she happened to get in the way, it would be easier to take care of both of them. You know, cars crash, people get killed. Happens every day."

The visitor put his hand down on the stop button.

"Heard enough?"

"That sorry bastard. Can I keep that tape? I should go to the police with it right now, before they have a chance to hurt anybody else. I want to see them both hang! I never trusted him. I always tried to tell Alicia about him."

"Ah, the dark side of wealth. No, I shouldn't even be here. I just thought you should know so that you could be on guard. The gentleman I work for, Mr. Pearlman, wants to play this tape at a special meeting of the board of directors before anyone else hears it. Let me ask you, since it was Mr. Pearlman who uncovered this, can he count on your support after all of this is over? You would then be in control of Alicia's stock."

"Tell Mr. Pearlman that I owe him and I will certainly remember this when he needs my help."

"Wonderful.

"You know, I don't even know your name."

"Aubrey, Aubrey Pryor. Well, this has certainly been informative. Please keep this under your hat for a few days. If anything should develop, I'll be in touch. Have a good evening."

"Thank you, Mr. Pryor. Thank you."

15

"Aaron, we've got to talk. I just got a call from a contact over at Frazier Smith."

"The stock exchange? What did they want?"

"Seems like your sister-in-law placed a call to Alicia's old agent and started asking about how many shares of voting stock she controls."

"Shit! This is getting worse by the second."

"Time is becoming a serious ingredient in this matter. Something drastic needs to happen soon."

"Does this come as some sort of surprise to you? You didn't think all of this newfound affection for her sister was just a guilty conscience, did you? This bitch is an alligator. She's a lot more dangerous than Pearlman could ever have been. She'll have us all in hell before this is over. And you're going to love this."

"What?"

"It seems that the Louisiana Police have found Alicia's kidnapper. Freda Payne called a short while ago. She left word for me at the office."

"How do they know it was him?"

"Supposedly, he felt the pressure of the authorities getting close to him. He wrote out a confession and blew his brains out."

"Do you think that's what happened?"

Burns paused before he answered. It was a negotiating technique he had learned years earlier as a young attorney. It made his adversaries cognizant of the fact that he studied every answer before offering it. Over the years, it had become second nature to him whenever the conversation turned serious.

"Like I said, we need to talk. God only knows what's in the confession. This can't be the guy I was dealing with. He just wasn't the type to blow his own brains out. I'll be in the office early in the morning, be there around 6 a.m. and we can talk before anyone else arrives."

"I'll be there. Fuck! There's nothing simple, is there?"

"In the morning."

* * *

Aaron Goldman could not sleep. Joan Williams had moved back to her own place in an effort to slow down the talk that was tearing the company apart. He wished she were there to hold on to as holding her and smelling her soft perfumed skin made sleep a lot easier. He knew now that Delores had designs of complete control of the destiny of Virginia Industrial. He had been an idiot to let her get close to Alicia. One thing for certain, he would never let her be appointed custodian by the court. He'd do whatever it took to keep her hands off those shares in the company. At two in the morning, after less than an hour's sleep, the phone beside the bed rang. Still groggy, he awoke immediately and listened to the incredible sounds on the phone.

"Oh... Jesus, Aaron. Help. Oh... Fuck... Stop... For Christ's sake you're killing me!" The cries for help were followed by another two full minutes of agonizing screams. Then there was silence. A moment later the phone disconnected. There was no mistaking the voice. It was Fred Burns. Under the present circumstances, Aaron felt he couldn't call the police. He would wait until morning and go to his scheduled meeting with Fred. If he didn't show up, that would be the time to call the authorities. The decision made, he tried to close his eyes and rest a short while. His anxiety and fear would not hear of it, so he lay on the bed, eyes fixed on the ceiling, unable to shut off his mind. As an afterthought, he got up, went to a dresser drawer and pulled out a snub-nosed thirty-eight caliber pistol and set it on the nightstand. He lay back down. Every noise in the house became a cause for concern. Would someone be coming for him as they had Burns? As he wondered about what he had just heard on the phone, it rang once again. He let it ring over a dozen times, not wanting to know who was calling. After all of the police's monitoring equipment was removed, he had not hooked his own answering machine back up. Finally, to end the ringing, he picked up the receiver. He was again subjected to another full minute of listening to Fred's screams. The calls continued every thirty minutes for the remainder of the night. By dawn, the screams had become an incoherent moan. There was no conscious thought left behind them.

* * *

Kathy Joseph and her daughter Chelsea were new to the neighborhood. Kathy's divorce had left her a single, working mother with a precocious daughter. He ex-husband had not accepted the demands of the court to provide child support and had only recently left the country so that no one would ever be able to force him to hand over another dime to the bitch he was convinced had ruined his life. They were on their own. Kathy found a job at a bakery in the city's commercial center downtown and a small apartment in an old brick home that had been carved up into rentals years before. They were worn out but in fairly safe part of the city. They would create a new life for themselves. Being an hourly employee with more expenses than income, Kathy worked as many hours as her employer would give her, never complaining or asking for time off. Chelsea was an independent twelve-year-old who usually made the right decision on things so her mother never worried much about her being home alone until she could get home from work. Chelsea would keep the doors locked and do her homework until her mother arrived. Many evenings she would have dinner started for her mother as she understood fully the sacrifice her mother was making to help them survive.

It was a little after 5 p.m. and Chelsea was home alone. Her mother had called to alert her that she was working a few extra hours this evening. "Bills are coming due at week's end and we really need the extra money. Will you be okay there 'til about eight? Can you fix yourself something to eat?"

"Don't worry about me, Mom. I'll get a bowl of cereal and get caught up on my homework until you get in. Mom, what are the chances we might be able to hook up cable soon? I really want to be able to see some of my favorite shows."

"I know baby. We'll see. I can't promise but we'll see. You be careful now and I'll be home shortly. And, Chelsea…"

"Yes, Mom?"

"Please keep the doors locked. I feel like our neighborhood is safe but it always pays to be careful."

"I will Mom. Don't worry about me."

"Okay, baby. Love you."

"You too."

Chelsea went to the old wooden cupboard and got out a box of cereal. She grabbed what was left of the milk from the fridge and sat down at the old dining table to eat. She missed her life in the suburbs with her dad at home and having enough money for things like a TV in her room and cable. She knew her mother and father had fought constantly and even though it was now a lot calmer at home, she missed her former life and friends. When she had moved to the new neighborhood in a lower rent district, a lot of her old friends went in different directions. At least her eyes were now open about who her real friends were. As she methodically ate her cereal, she reminisced about how things used to be, how happy she was. Above the noise of the old furnace blower she began to hear a new sound, almost like a baby crying. She followed the noise to the window overlooking the old brick building adjoining hers. It was hard to hear over the blower so she went to the wall where the thermostat was hung and cut off the fan. Back at the window she strained to determine what the noise was. It just might be a puppy that some neighbor didn't want and turned out to face life on its own. She would love to have a puppy. That would give her the companion she wanted so desperately. It did sound as though it might be a puppy. It wasn't quite dark outside so she went out the back door and around to the side yard. Again, she heard the same soft cry. It was definitely coming from the neighbor's house, but not the yard. The sound was coming from the basement. There was a small basement window on the side of the house so she walked over to it only to discover it was painted black from the inside. She pressed her head up close to the darkened window and now she could distinctly hear the sound. It wasn't a baby or a puppy. It was someone crying out in pain. It reminded her of the painful cries she heard the night she spent in the emergency room after she broke her ankle skating. It was someone in a great deal of pain. She went to the front door to alert the owner that there was certainly a problem with someone living there. If there were no answer she would go home and call 911 to bring help.

Kathy arrived home just at 8 p.m. that evening. Most evenings when she arrived after working late, Chelsea would be there to greet her at the door. She would open it for her mother before she could get the house key out of her purse. That was not the case this evening. She assumed that her daughter must be reading or heavily into her homework. Her grades had suffered some due to the uprooting from her previous school. It would be wonderful if she took some interest in her courses. Kathy walked down the hall to the kitchen.

"Chelsea, I'm home, baby. Did you get yourself something to eat?"

Kathy went into the kitchen and was surprised to see the almost-full soggy bowl of cold cereal sitting on the table. The milk had been out and was sitting beside it. She reached out to grab the milk jug to place back in the fridge and was shaken when she realized how warm it was. It had obviously been sitting out for quite a while.

"Chelsea, where are you?"

No answer. She walked to the back door and grew even more concerned when she realized it was shut but not locked. She looked out at the now dark yard.

"Chelsea, are you out here?"

Again, no answer. Full-fledged panic now struck Kathy in her gut. Something was drastically wrong. Chelsea was not a kid who would worry her mother or play games with her. She quickly went through the entire apartment calling out for her daughter as she ran. In less than a minute Kathy had determined she was not in the house nor in the yard. Kathy grabbed her phone from her purse and immediately dialed 911.

"This is 911, what is the nature of your emergency?"

"My daughter. She was home by herself for just a short time while I was working and she is gone. She's nowhere to be found."

"Yes, ma'am. What makes you think she's missing? Could she be next door or at a friend's house?"

"No. She doesn't have any friends here. We just moved in a couple weeks ago and we don't know anybody here. I tell you something bad has happened to her."

"Okay, ma'am. What is your name and address? I'll send over an officer to see you."

By the time the police car pulled up to the front of the house, Kathy was close to a complete meltdown. Two uniformed officers searched the house and yard thoroughly.

"Ma'am. She's definitely not here."

"That's what I've been telling you. Someone has taken her."

"You say you're recently divorced. Was there a custody dispute? Do you think your ex-husband might have taken her?"

"No chance. He's hiding out so he won't have to pay child support. He doesn't want to see either of us ever again. He made that very clear. I think he's in Australia."

"There's no forced entry. Either your daughter... You say her name is Chelsea?"

"Yes, that's correct."

"Either Chelsea let someone in the house that she knew or was not afraid of or she went outside on her own."

"We don't know anyone here. I'm sure she didn't let anyone in. She must have gone outside for some reason."

"Okay. We'll canvas the neighbors and see if anyone saw anything unusual. Will you be alright until we get back?"

"Please, just go. I'll stay here in case she shows back up."

Doctor K was in no way surprised when the officers showed up at the front door.

"Good evening officers. What can I help you with?"

"Sir, are you the owner here?"

"That's right. What's the problem?"

"A young girl, twelve years old is missing. She lives right next door. Have you seen or heard anything that might help us find her?"

"Goodness, I thought that house was empty. The last I remembered it was in such bad shape I'm surprised anyone could live there. Of course, I've been away on business quite a lot recently. Someone could have moved in while I was away. And no, to your question. It's been very quiet here all evening. I've been just inside in the living room reading the newspaper. Surely I would have heard if there had been a problem nearby."

"Thanks sir. Please let us know if you think of anything."

"I will, officers; I certainly will. Come to think of it, there was one thing that comes to mind. It was about two hours ago. A van, dark green was parked just out front between our houses. I didn't think anything of it at the time. A lot of cars park there as there is so little parking on the street. But I was surprised at how much noise it made when they pulled out. It squealed the tires. I just thought it might be some local gang members or a teenager in their daddy's car, if you know what I mean. They really hit the pedal when they left. Might not mean a thing but I thought I should mention it to you."

"Yes, sir. I'll make a note here. You didn't get a plate number, did you?"

"No, sorry. I didn't. It did have some writing on the side though."

"Do you remember what it said?"

"It might have been a plumber or no, wait... Maybe a cleaner. I'm sorry. I just didn't pay it much attention at the time."

"If you remember anything else, sir, please give us a call."

"Count on it. And officers..."

"Yes, sir?"

"I certainly hope you find the child. I love children and it pains me to think so many are growing up in such a dangerous world."

"Thank you, sir."

"No problem. Good evening, officers."

After a couple more hours of making the rounds with no luck, the officers returned to speak with Kathy. By this time there was another pair of officers in the house. They were plainclothes detectives and it was clear that they expected the worst. One detective was a middle-aged woman with short grey hair and a very tired face. She was Karen Martin, a twenty-two year veteran of the force and the local expert on missing persons, especially children. She took Kathy's hand as she spoke with her.

"I know this is incredibly hard for you, Kathy. But we have to ask you every question we can think of that might help us find Chelsea. I've handled many cases like this and we have a good record of finding missing children within a few hours. I'm praying that this will have such an ending. I won't quit until we find your daughter. I have a daughter myself so I can put myself in your shoes."

"Karen, I'll do anything you want. I'll quit my job and work full-time searching for her. Anything you think will help."

"I know Kathy. The main thing you can do is stay strong. Have faith we will find her. If she doesn't turn up tonight, then by morning we need to post pictures of her all over the community with her vitals on it so folks in the area will know who to look for and that she is missing."

"I'll be here on the couch all night. I'll have one ready to go by sunrise."

"Okay. We're going to leave an officer here with you all night as well in case you need help or in case she tries to contact you in some fashion. Don't lose faith. We'll find her."

The coming nights would pass slowly, painfully slow. The next day, the next night, and the following week would pass by with no word or clues as to what happened to Chelsea. A grief-ridden Kathy confined herself to her bed, unable to go to work or function in any manner.

* * *

"Mornin', Mr. Goldman. Ain't you here awful early today?"

The security guard smiled as he waited for an answer. "Has Mr. Burns arrived yet?"

"I just come on at six; hadn't come in since then. Unless he was here before that, I ain't seen him."

Aaron knew when he had to unlock the glass door leading down the hall to the executive offices that no one else was there. Just to be certain, he checked Burns' office anyway. As expected, he found it empty. There was a post-it stuck to his door that a secretary had placed there after Burns had left for the day. Aaron removed the note, which had only the line "Call Freda Payne" and her phone number. He went to his own office and sat down, trying to make sense out of the events of the previous evening. By 10 a.m., there was still no word from Fred Burns. After trying his home and car phones all morning, Aaron decided to go to the Burnses house. He could not bring himself to be the one to call the authorities. Though he was certain that something sinister had happened to Fred, he wanted to be told about it by someone else. No need to raise any red flags for the police. Any thoughts of Aaron being a suspect in Alicia's kidnapping had long before been dismissed and he wanted to keep all that behind him. Could Burns have been involved in anything else worthy of someone torturing him? If not, this all had to be tied to their handling of Alicia's disappearance. It couldn't be a matter of loyalty. Fred Burns was the only link to him and Fred loved his power position in the company too much to ever betray their arrangement.

Nothing seemed out of place from the front yard. The door was locked and no one answered the bell or Aaron's repeated knocking. The only thing that gave rise to suspicion was Burns' BMW still sitting in the drive. Aaron slipped around to the back yard and pulled on the handle of the French door that led to the back deck. It opened easily. Aaron walked in the back door which opened to the kitchen. The radio on the intercom was playing classical music in every room. Aaron made his way from room to room, winding up at the door to the master bedroom.

Feeling a great amount of apprehension, he pushed open the door. His dread was well-founded. Under the coverings on the bed there appeared to be someone lying curled up in a fetal position. He pulled the colorful quilt back to reveal a white, silk sheet completely soaked with blood. His heart raced and he looked behind him to make certain he was alone. He turned back and gave a hard pull on the sheet, throwing it completely to the foot of the king-sized bed. There, curled up and lying face down, with her head toward the foot of the bed was Diane Burns. She was bloodied from head to toe. This was not what he had been expecting and he could feel the contents of his already-disturbed stomach rising to the back of his throat. Aaron pushed on the side of her head revealing, among her other many wounds, that her throat had been slit. It was almost severed on the left side. In the few spots where her skin was not smeared with her own blood, her color was a dull white, like a dead fish. Cold to the touch, it was apparent that she had been dead for quite some time.

He quickly found the toilet adjoining the bedroom and heaved his guts into the bowl. Not wanting to leave any residue of his presence there, he wiped off the rim with toilet paper and flushed the contents. He returned to where Diane Burns lay in her grotesquely contorted death position. His mind racing and feeling that his sins were following too close behind him, he didn't know whether to call the police or not. He continued to search the house for Fred but there was no trace. Whoever had killed Diane Burns had taken Fred. The sound of Fred's screams over the phone replayed in his mind.

He quickly left the way he had entered, being careful to disturb nothing as he moved. Who... And why, would anyone want to kill them? Aaron's mind reeled as he drove home. Was it time to come clean? He knew it would be the end of life as he knew it. It would surely lead to a lengthy stretch in prison, almost certainly life. He hadn't personally harmed anyone. Technically, he had just been a co-conspirator. Hell, for that matter, Burns was the real brain behind the entire scheme. Maybe it would all just pass and Aaron would be left with no traceable connections to anything. Burns could be the fall guy. But who killed the two of them? The murderer must know what Fred and Aaron had been up to. Thus, for this to work, he would have to learn who had killed the Burnses – assuming Fred was also dead – and exactly what they knew.

* * *

The abduction of Chelsea was starting to get a lot of press. The local news ran a special on exploited children and featured her. All the attention was forcing the authorities to assign more personnel to the case. To a department already strapped for funding and personnel, it was hard to allocate so much resource to a single case. But bad press was something the local District Attorney did not want to deal with in an election year. He made it very clear to everyone that finding this child would be their number one goal. Freda Payne had been placed in charge of the investigation.

* * *

The basement of Doctor K's home was basically a cell. He had altered its interior to resemble an emergency room lab but no mistake could be made about it. It was most certainly a prison. The chairs all contained hooks for attaching straps. The doors between rooms were reinforced steel and the locks were identical to those used in prisons. Once inside, a 'guest' would remain there until he was ready to let them move on, out, or into the ethereal world. Chelsea regained consciousness inside one of these rooms. At only twelve, it was particularly frightening.

"Ah, my sweet young and very curious neighbor. What is your name, young lady?"

"I'm Chelsea, Chelsea Joseph. Where am I? Is this a hospital? Did I get hurt?"

"No, you didn't get hurt. I think that perhaps you must have fainted just outside in my yard, next to a window. I found you there and brought you inside before you caught your death of cold."

"I remember. I heard someone crying in your basement. You need to go check it out. Someone down there is really hurt bad."

"I'm afraid you are mistaken, Miss Chelsea. We are, at this very moment, in my basement and as you can see, we are quite alone. Perhaps you heard a program on my television in another room."

"No. It was real. I know it was real. And, I don't think I passed out. I never faint. Somebody must have knocked me out."

"Very interesting. Well, Miss Chelsea. I don't know what to tell you. We are the only people that are down here. You say you and your mother live alone next door?"

"Yes. My daddy left us and now it's just us. We had to move from our big new house to this old one 'cause we don't have any money to have a nice one."

"Most unfortunate. Seems to be the sign of the times, families breaking up. What's your mother's name? I'll certainly need to get in touch with her and let her know you're over here."

"No need, Mr.... I don't know your name."

"My name is Kale, Spencer Kale. I'm a doctor."

"What kind of doctor are you?"

"I specialize in pain management. I try to help people with their suffering."

"That's very nice. It's not good to hurt. I broke my ankle and it really hurt."

"It's a shame we didn't know each other back then. I most certainly could have helped you."

"Well, Doctor Kale. I better get on back home now. I'm sure my mother is worried. How do I get out of here?"

"Chelsea, you need to let me go get your mother for you. When you fainted you were out for some time and I don't want to alarm her. I'll just go over to your house and bring her back with me. You'll need to wait here while I handle that little matter."

"No, I want to see my mother. I'll go with you." Chelsea was beginning to realize that all was not what it had originally seemed. This was not just a kindly old doctor trying to help her. "I really need to get home. I'm sure my mother is worried sick about me."

"No doubt, Chelsea. But I'll take care of all that. You will need to stay here though. And goodness, that seems to be a real nasty bruise on your face."

Chelsea reached up to feel her face. "Where, I don't feel anything."

"It's right over here, just to the side of your nose. There's a little dried blood there. Here, I'll get it with this little cloth."

"Doctor K reached over with a small cloth smothered in ether. After less than five seconds of struggle, Chelsea was lying still on an examining table in the room. Doctor K looked at her lying there, connected her arms and legs to the table with straps and smiled as he left the room.

"Now, let's go meet Miss Kathy, shall we?" he muttered to himself. Doctor K left the basement and grabbed a jacket from the hall closet. As he opened the door to go next door he spotted a uniformed policeman standing by Kathy Joseph's front door. There was also a squad car parked out front. At that moment a grey, unmarked sedan pulled up out front and Freda Payne stepped out accompanied by two other plainclothes detectives. They greeted the officer at the front door, who opened it for them. Freda went inside. Doctor K turned and immediately went back inside too. He would have to come up with a new plan.

Freda looked directly into Kathy's worn eyes. "How are you doing, hon?"

"Not well. I don't know how much longer I can hold on. Chelsea is all I have."

"I understand. I do have some good news for you."

"I can certainly use some. What's going on?"

"We are about to begin the largest missing person hunt this city has ever seen. We are going to go door-to-door through the neighborhood in the morning and canvass in detail everyone who lives around here. We will find out what happened. We have already located a gas station at one end of your street and a market on the other that both had video cameras trained on the outside at the time Chelsea disappeared. We also got approval to enlist the help of one of the country's most accomplished investigators. His name is Aubrey Pryor and he is absolutely brilliant in solving these cases. He will be here in the morning.

With dawn came an army of police to Kathy Joseph's front door. Freda walked over to Kathy and introduced her to Aubrey. Kathy, I'd like you to meet Aubrey Pryor.

"Nice to meet you, sir. I certainly hope you can help me find Chelsea."

"I'm going to give it my best shot. I've been given a copy of your statements and the police reports from all the officers. I'm expecting a call from our office any minute with the results of the security video tapes from the local station and market. Within moments the call came in that he had just mentioned. Aubrey asked to talk with the investigator examining the tapes.

"Nothing, eh? Nothing suspicious during the hours we need? What about the green van the neighbor mentioned?"

"That's very odd. Unless it stopped on the same block and spent the night, it should have been on the tape. Okay, I'll look into that from this end."

Aubrey turned to Freda. "I think we need to go next door and speak to this Doctor Spencer. The green van he reported squealing out of here apparently never made it to either end of this block. Something is definitely amiss. How about letting me take a couple of officers with me while I speak with this gentleman?"

"No problem. Grab a couple from out front and they can accompany you."

Aubrey and two armed patrol officers approached the home of Doctor Kale Spencer. There was no car in the drive and the place seemed to be shut up entirely. Aubrey motioned to the officers.

"One of you go around back and make sure nobody leaves the house. The other can come with me and let's see if anybody's home."

Aubrey rang the doorbell several times to no avail. Thinking it may not be working he started to knock on the door, first with normal force and soon with very substantial energy. Still there was no answer. Aubrey looked at the policeman. "And what if I think someone may be inside in danger, do I need a search warrant?"

"Detective Payne said to find the kid. Stand back and I'll see if I can knock on the door with a little more force." The officer kicked the door twice before the deadbolt finally parted from the wooden frame and swung open. There were no lights on inside. It was stone, cold quiet. The officer with Aubrey went down the hall and opened the back door so the other officer could come in as well. By now they were on their handheld radios requesting additional support. In less than a minute ten officers were going through the house, searching every closet, nook and corner.

"Nothing, Mr. Pryor. The place looks like a museum. Everything is set up like they're getting ready to do a House and Garden photo shoot. Nothing's out of order."

Aubrey went over to the main hall closet, opened the door and walked to the back. "Feel that?"

"What sir? I don't feel nothing."

"Put your hand right here."

"What am I supposed to be looking for?"

"Feel the draft? There's a small crack in the back of the closet. I'm willing to bet this wall here…" Aubrey pulled out three shoe boxes from the adjacent shelf and revealed a small button on the wall. He pushed it and the back of the closet swung open like a door. Aubrey reached inside and found a light switch. He flipped the switch and the light revealed a staircase leading to a basement, which they all descended.

"I knew this place had to have a basement. There's a blackened window out to the side next to Mrs. Joseph's house. I'm willing to bet that Chelsea saw or heard something that brought her over here and I hope we're not too late." With an officer beside him, gun in hand, Aubrey opened each of three doors that opened onto the center hall they were in. Each room was dark and as they found the light switches it became very apparent that the neighbor was not an ordinary physician.

"I've got a very sick feeling about this. This looks more like an operating room than a basement."

Other than equipment, each of the first two rooms was empty. As they entered the last door and cut on the overhead light, a small gurney with a body on it covered by a sheet was seen in the center of the space. Aubrey walked over to the sheet and pulled it back revealing Chelsea. He felt her neck for a pulse.

"It's faint but still there. She's alive!"

Kathy Joseph heard all the commotion coming from the house next door. She knew it had to be in connection to Chelsea so she slipped on a housecoat and practically ran to the front lawn. As she drew closer she saw Aubrey carrying the young girl, still wrapped in a sheet in his arms. With tears streaming down her face and her heart racing she ran to him. "Is she? Is she?"

Aubrey smiled. "She's fine. She's been drugged but she's alive and seems unharmed. She was there alone. Whoever took her really had no use for her and left her there for us to find."

Freda came over as well and asked Aubrey, "Can she talk? Can she tell us who did this?"

"I'm willing to bet we will get nothing from her."

"Why is that?"

Aubrey reached into his pocket and pulled out a small medicine vial. "This was on the counter next to her. It's Flunitrazepam."

"What the hell is that?"

"Doctors use it to help patients forget traumatic events and even surgery. It basically produces amnesia, kind of like the date rape drug, only much more effective. She'll be lucky to remember anything prior to last week if my guess is correct. But she is alive and seems to be unharmed. Perhaps I'm wrong but we'll see when she comes to. Mrs. Joseph, how about you and Freda take your daughter back to your house? I want to go back next door and check out this madman's den."

Kathy ran over to Aubrey and hugged him so tightly it almost took his breath away. "I'll always be indebted to you. If there is ever anything I can do for you, just call. No matter what I'll always owe you for giving me my child's life back, and mine."

"You don't owe me anything, Kathy. Finding Chelsea and solving cases like this is the only reward I want. I'm thrilled with the outcome. You go on home now and get her inside out of the cold."

Aubrey went back over to Doctor K's lair and spent the rest of the morning going over every inch with the most trained eyes to ever visit a crime scene. He would meet with Freda later that afternoon.

* * *

"Freda, I'm very alarmed by what I found here. There is no doubt that this home, lab, torture chamber; whatever you want to call it, has been set up for quite a while. This is the handiwork of a very sophisticated serial killer. The lab technicians have been looking the site over for half a day and haven't found even a partial fingerprint, nothing that could be traced back to a single individual. The neighbors say a kindly looking, non-descript old man lived there and he almost never set foot outside. He drove a plain brown sedan and never drew any attention from anyone. I think we should go as far back as the past year and carefully look at every video from the two stores that they have on file. Maybe we can pick out the brown sedan by eliminating all the other cars on the street from the footage. Other than that, it will be a miracle if we find him. Trust me, he knows we're onto him and he is long gone by now."

Freda paced the floor as she spoke. "Okay. We need to go to the Register of Deeds office and find out who owns the place. He's probably a renter but perhaps they'll have something to offer us."

"Don't count on it. This guy is sick but smart. You can count on the renter's ID being faked and I'm sure in this part of town the owner was more than happy to rent to anyone with cash. From the amount of equipment and the looks of the chamber in the basement, this guy does have a source of funding. He's not a street person."

"Why do you suppose he left Chelsea unharmed?"

"She doesn't fit some profile that he has in his head. Who knows, he could have a soft spot for kids. The mind of someone like this is far removed from normal logic. I normally just look for patterns and try to determine what scenario they're following in their twisted minds. I get on the same track they're on and sometimes I can determine what they're up to and where to look for them. This guy is different though. I don't know a lot about his motivation to do what he does, but I assure you I will before I'm done. I'm just thankful we could bring Kathy's child back to her."

"In my book, Aubrey, you are the hero here. Thank you for what you do."

"Not a problem. I get a lot of satisfaction from solving these crimes."

* * *

The phone in Goldman's office was ringing when he arrived.

"Mr. Goldman?"

"Yes. Who is this?"

"It's Aubrey Pryor, Mr. Goldman. I just had a pretty bizarre phone call and I thought I better get up with you. I believe you could be in danger. And do you know how to get up with Mr. Burns? I've been trying to contact him all morning."

"No. I've been looking for him myself. Do you have any idea who made the call?"

"No. But I did record it. Can you meet with me and listen to it? Maybe you'll have some idea who it is. One thing for certain though, whoever did this, is a brick short of a load."

"This morning, nothing surprises me. Where would you like to meet?"

"One hour. The Tobacco Road Grill on Broad Street. You know where it is?"

"Yes. I'll be there."

Aaron parked in the city lot across the street from the grill. The grill, a local favorite, was located in downtown Richmond and like any other workday, a parking spot was difficult to find. He started to cross the street and as he stepped down from the curb, a brown sedan came to a stop directly in front of him.

The passenger door opened. "Get in, Mr. Goldman. Sorry I'm late. The grill looks packed. I know a place a little less crowded this time of day."

Aaron sat down on the front seat opposite Aubrey Pryor.

"You have the tape with you?"

"Right here. We'll get a cup of coffee and take a listen. You know, all this rain is depressing, isn't it? I'm ready to see the sun again. I'm hoping this could be the break we've been waiting for. If you recognize the voice, we'll know where to look. This has been about the most peculiar case I've ever been on. Just haven't been any leads to follow. Very unusual. At least your wife seems to be getting better, I hear. That's wonderful."

"Yes, we're real pleased with how well she's doing."

"I'm sure. Damn! This is the place I wanted to stop at. It's full too. How about I just run in and grab two cups of coffee and we can take them to my office and listen to the thing there?"

"You have an office close by?"

"It's just several blocks from here. Down by the old bus station."

"Sounds fine. Let's just get a move on though. I'm running behind."

"I'll be right back. I'll just leave the motor running."

Aaron was growing tired, yet he was too frightened by the possible consequences of this entire turn of events to give up now. He would follow through with this scenario until it came to a conclusion. He would not allow his fear to overcome his own best interest. As of now, everyone was on their own. He would look out for himself at all costs. Damn anyone who tried to attack him.

Moments later, the rotund little investigator returned, two Styrofoam cups in hand. "Here. Jeez, I'm drenched. I hope this coffee is hot. Hate cold coffee."

As they approached the block where Aubrey's office was located, he pulled over to the curb. "This is about as close as we're gonna get a spot. We can just make a run for it. You okay? You don't look so good."

"I'm beginning to feel real nauseous. I haven't had anything to eat today and this coffee is not setting well on my empty stomach. Damn, I'm not feeling very good."

16

"Delores, are we going to go out again today? I'm feeling soooo good! I think that the methadone is going to work. It's almost like I have been living with my mind in a fog. I'm beginning to remember so many things."

"You don't know how happy I am to know that I have my sister back. You have a doctor's appointment at four this afternoon. We can go to lunch, maybe drop by our favorite auction house, Furman's, and then to the doctor. You look pretty this morning. I think you're going to be just as good as new, Alicia."

Alicia focused as she spoke. Her words were not as quick to leave her mouth as before her abduction, but they indicated a much improved intellect and awareness compared to just a few short weeks and months ago. "You'll never know what I went through, Delores. I try not to even think about it, but it's hard. At least the nightmares have stopped. Maybe one day things will be like before. And... Delores..."

"Yes?"

"What about Aaron? Why doesn't he come see me? Do I... Do I look so bad that he can't bring himself to look at me? I know I'm not very attractive anymore."

"You are, baby. Don't think that for a moment. You have to remember. Aaron thought you were dead. He was in agony over your disappearance for a very long time. It's got to be hard for him to adjust to your return. I'm sure he'll come around. Let me ask you something. If, and just if, he was unable to face this turnaround..."

"You mean and not want me back?"

"For whatever reason."

"I would be terribly disappointed, but I would deal with it. He might not even want me if he knew..."

"That you had a woman for a lover?"

"Yes. Do you think he could deal with that?"

"I don't know, Alicia, I just don't know. A lot of men would have a problem there. It's funny, you know. What drove us apart for so long is actually bringing us together now. I hate that our father had such a hard time dealing with it, but hey. No need to talk of all these heavy things right now. Throw some clothes on and let's get over to Furman's before all the good stuff has been picked over."

* * *

"Mr. Goldman. Aaron. Are you awake? Do you hear me, Aaron?"

"Aubrey, what happened? Where are we?"

"We're at my home, Aaron. You were out for quite some time. How are you feeling?"

"Head hurts, terribly. I must have passed out. I was feeling so sick. Hadn't slept any."

"Not exactly, Aaron. You have been out some time now, due to a fairly strong dosage of a powdered anesthetic."

"You mean someone intentionally drugged me?"

"Exactly."

"Why would they do that?"

"There's no 'they' to it, Aaron. Just me."

"You? But why would you drug me?"

Aaron tried to reach up to his head and found his arms and legs securely fastened to the chair that he was sitting in.

"My priorities have changed."

"Why am I strapped in this chair? Undo these straps, Aubrey."

"No can do, Aaron. You're going to be with me here for a while."

"Okay, it's pretty fucking obvious that you've been bought off. Whatever you've been promised, I'll beat it. I thought you were a straight guy, Aubrey. Now, I see you're just like everybody else. Show you a buck and you'll sell out instantly."

"Nothing could be further from the truth."

"You haven't taken a better offer?"

"Well, there's actually some truth there. I was responding to your remark about me being just like everybody else. As far as I can tell, there's no one quite like me. And, that's probably a very good thing for society. And now, about the predicament that you find yourself in."

"What do you want? If money isn't what turns you on, what is it you want?"

"You. I want you and as you can see, I have you. And as far as selling out, I don't have to. I've been on retainer to all of your adversaries from day one."

"Who are you talking about?"

"For openers, Ernest Pearlman. And your beloved sister-in-law and even Fred Burns. They all were very satisfied with my efforts."

"About Burns. Where the hell is he?"

"I terminated his position as my employer. He was a very bright guy. You know, he was the one who brought me into all this to start with. He offered a quite large sum of money to arrange for your wife's... Well let's just call it her restructuring."

"You... You were the one who kidnapped Alicia?"

"Bingo! And you, you were so kind to pay me to find her. I could hardly believe it when I got the call. A stroke of genius. You not only hire the best private investigator possible, you wind up with the one guy who could never succeed in that endeavor. Pearlman, of course wanted all the dirt he could get on you and your sister-in-law. What a piece of work you have there."

"What about her?"

"Well, that's why you're here today. For some reason, she was able to determine just who it was that caused all of the unfortunate problems for poor Alicia."

"Oh, she just guessed. That's what you're saying?"

"An educated guess. And, she was very upset with you. She seems to feel that if you're not there, she can vote Alicia's stock and use her own rather hefty stash of green to buy out Mr. Pearlman. It seems like everyone wins. Everyone but you, of course. But getting back to Burns. I get so excited thinking about him that I can hardly stand it. You didn't know this, but Mr. Burns first came to me to help him with an accounting problem at your firm. Seems that a certain David Enright ascertained that Burns had relieved the company of a great deal of cash."

"I don't believe that for a moment. He had no reason to steal. Hell, he was making a fortune without stealing."

"Please don't interrupt me again, Aaron. You don't want to upset me with your poor manners this early in our little venture. Well, I saw to it that poor Mr. Enright took a short boat ride away from his calculator. Of course, he had actually perished several days prior to that little accident. You're going to be the first person, other than me of course, to find out what happened to him. Kind of exciting, huh?"

"You're out of your mind!"

"Please, you're so melodramatic, Aaron. Now where was I? Oh yes, I was talking about Fred Burns and his new career."

"New career? You mean he's still alive?"

"Why, of course. And poor Diane Burns, I wish I could have had more time with her, but everything doesn't always work out the way we want."

"You did that to her? You're so fucking crazy it's sad."

"Last warning, Aaron. Now as I was saying, I have been helping Fred to prepare himself for a whole new life, actually. Just a second, he's right back here. I'm sure he'd like to see you. Well, that's not really possible, but you can certainly see him."

Doctor K moved away behind Aaron and in a few seconds he could hear the squeak of small wheels as on a grocery cart coming toward him. What appeared before him literally took his breath away. Seated upright, strapped in a wheelchair was his longtime friend and lawyer. Emaciated and pale, his eyes seemed to be wandering separately from each other and he drooled from the mouth like a palsy victim.

"Oh, fuck! What have you done to him?"

"Haven't you ever heard the old saying ignorance is bliss? Fred Burns is now an extremely happy man. I have this rather unique technique I developed for reducing the oxygen flow through the carotid artery to the cerebrum. I can almost measure the intelligence reduction by the look in my patient's eyes. I'd say old Fred here is down to about fifty or so. You know, a smart chimpanzee has about a fifty IQ. Quite a change from the hundred and fifty plus he possessed on his way through Harvard Law

School, wouldn't you say? He can still hear just a little, but alas, he doesn't seem to comprehend a great deal. Watch this!"

He reached over and scratched Burns on the neck. The pathetic mound of flesh gave an asymmetrical, now toothless, no-comprehension grin, much like an extremely retarded child might.

"That's so cute. Don't you think so, Mr. Goldman? It's the intention of those paying for his treatment, and yours I might add, that Fred Burns spend the rest of his days on a small cart in the heart of the financial district, selling pencils from a cup and most important of all, enjoying it. Hey look. He's happy. Am I right? Delores wants to be able to pass by him every morning on her way to her office as the new Chairman of Virginia Industrial and throw a quarter to him. She absolutely radiates just talking about you and Burns. Just the thought of him sitting at that corner and having his old colleagues pass him by without so much as a second glance is mind-numbing. It makes me feel like a God.

"Over the next couple of days, I'm going to have to remove his legs and make sure that he has only minimal control over his hands and none, of course over his bowels. She was very specific about that. And I'll have more enjoyment getting old Freddie to this point than you'll ever understand, but enough about Burns. Let's address your future, Aaron. Both the near future and the long-term. You are to be a masterpiece. Your wonderful sister-in-law – I love her to death – is paying me a small fortune to perform a miracle on you. Of course, they think they're dealing with good old Aubrey Pryor. A middleman you might say."

Aaron Goldman listened, his mind in a mixed state of disbelief, confusion, and fear. It would be easy to imagine this to be some sort of sick joke if the destroyed remains of Fred Burns were not sitting five feet in front of him, smiling at the sounds in front of him in incomprehensible bliss.

"And me... What are you planning on doing with me?"

"Not with you, Aaron. To you. You are in for quite an adventure. You saw what a dramatic change I was able to bring about in Alicia and Burns? That's really small compared to what I have in mind for you. Yes, you are headed on a remarkable journey. Your benefactors want you to experience what your beloved wife went through while she was in my care and see if you can respond with as much grace as she did. You are going to become, in short order, a completely different person than who you are right now. First, you are going to fall in love with heroin, just as Alicia did, and while you are developing that taste, we are going to realign your gender so that your services as a prostitute will be more in demand."

"You're mad, completely insane! You..."

Doctor K removed a large piece of adhesive tape from a roll and placed it over Aaron's mouth. "Sorry about that, Aaron. I promise you that I will never do it again. After tonight, I won't have to. You're going to be a lot quieter by tomorrow. I do this wonderful thing with a tongue...

"Okay, now back to your future. Tomorrow, right after the castration, we'll get you started on a really neat combination of estrogen and lead. We're going to start gentling you down and realigning your mental capacities all at the same time. And now, let's bring a gurney over here and see can't we get started. Yes sir, sometimes I have to pinch myself to see if I'm merely dreaming or that I truly have been so blessed."

Doctor K reached behind Aaron's head and pulled up a section of table and then pushed him back in a prone position. He then picked up the foot section and made certain that Aaron was strapped securely in the reclining position.

"First, we need to get you physically more inclined to participate in this little experiment. Here, let's remove this tape from your mouth now. It's in the way, you might say."

Aaron gasped for air as the tape was removed. Almost simultaneously he spoke in a breathless, excited flurry. "Aubrey, come on now, I always respected your ability. Why can't we just make a deal of some sort?"

"You need to call me Doctor K. That's short for Kale, my given name."

Doctor K pulled a long section of adhesive tape off a role and taped Aaron's head down. He then produced a surgical tray containing the same assortment of tools he had used in his initial procedures on David Enright. He taped Aaron's mouth in an open position and held the forceps over his head.

"This is one of my favorite treatments, Aaron. Incidentally, your lawyer buddy, Burns didn't handle this well at all."

17

Spring had been a long time coming. Richmond, with its dogwood-lined streets and antebellum homes looked like a scene out of a William Faulkner novel. It would be easy to imagine Big Daddy sitting in his wicker rocker on the front porch of some columned estate, fanning himself while a youngster went to fetch him a mint julep. Just past the end of Monument Avenue, was the historic business district with many storefronts dating back to the late 1800s. There were many chic boutiques and high-end eateries where Richmond's elite dined and socialized.

The Board of Directors was gathering at Shocko Seventeen for an elaborate luncheon celebration of the selection of Delores Thompson to be the new Chairman of Virginia Industrial. Most of the members were already in the private dining room sampling the champagne when Delores' stretch limo pulled alongside the curb in front of the prestigious location.

Her sister Alicia, and her new love Carolyn, were accompanying Delores to the meeting. Alicia, looking very smart in her business suit with a bobbed hairdo and obvious butch persona, was only too pleased to allow her sister to vote her stock. She had her life back, minus her bastard husband, and with the deep love that only another woman could offer her now. She and Delores now saw life from the same window.

As they exited and the driver closed the door behind them, Delores turned to the others. "Let's walk to the end of this street if you don't mind. You know how I hate to come this far into town and not stop by my favorite spot in the entire downtown area."

"Certainly. I think we all enjoy this little diversion equally." Alicia grabbed her girlfriend's arm as they walked and squeezed it affectionately. Carolyn reached in her purse and retrieved two cigarettes which she lit for herself and Alicia. They laughed and carried on with small talked as they walked to the corner. There, sitting on a small wooden pallet wearing a tattered overcoat, a wool stocking cap pulled down over most of his bearded face sat Fred Burns. He was propped up against the bricks on the front of the bank building where he once commanded great respect as a valued customer and mover and shaker in the community. No one who passed him by as he sat there, cup in hand, the legless beggar on the street corner, would ever know who this pathetic creature used to be. No one, that is except the three women who approached him.

"Why Freddie Burns, you sweet thing. Do you have much change in your cup today, honey? I know you're happy that winter has finally gone away so you don't have to sit out here all bundled up in the snow. It can be so cold here in the winter. I do think that before this summer is over I'm going to try to get one of the agencies here in the city to try and help you find some warmer clothes to wear. We don't want you to freeze to death and not be able to warm our hearts with your presence each time we come down here to eat. It means so much to us all. Here darling, let Delores put a little something in your cup."

She reached in her purse and pulled out some loose change and dropped the coins one at a time in the cup. Burns, never showing any real comprehension as to what was going on, just kept smiling and quietly whispering. "Thank you, thank you. Fred thanks you. Thanks, thanks…"

As they turned to walk back to the restaurant Delores took one last look back. "I can't tell you what that does for me. I can come down here and be totally stressed out and just seeing him that way… Well, it makes me feel all giddy. Now, what do you ladies say we go to greet my directors and receive my crown?"

The ladies continued up the street, walking briskly and chatting as they went away.

* * *

Bangkok is one of the most outlandish places on the globe, sexually speaking. Brothels occupy entire floors of downtown office buildings and sexual pleasures of every variety are offered openly in store windows. It would be hard to shock anyone with any carnal deviation in Bangkok.

Still, the Spider Club was on the fringe, even for this city. Even the authorities, openly tolerant of almost every sort of sexual vice, considered the Spider Club to be just about more than the city could allow. It was frequented by patrons who needed gratification from fetishes far removed from the mainstream deviant. There were straights with weird requirements, gays with far out needs, cross dressers and transsexuals and every other sexual permutation anyone could ever imagine. Even so, it was always full. Every night it was standing room only. Just behind the large bar and meeting room were a series of small rooms used to allow sex professionals to ply their trade, unfettered by societal norms. Some were freelance, sharing their income with the club for the right to be there and occupy a small room. Others were part of a much larger affair, that of organized crime, seedy businessmen, and pimps. Anything that ever crossed your mind, even your wildest desires could be purchased or rented at the Spider Club. The overweight, barrel-chested longshoreman strode to the bar and ordered a straight shot of bourbon. Over sixty and not in any way concerned about his appearance, he downed the shot in one swallow and followed it with three more. He turned to the bartender. "I got a question for you."

"Another shot, sir?"

"Naw, I'm running out of money and anyway I got something else I want. I need some special treatment if you get my drift. I'm told you have a very interesting woman working here. They said her name was Ariana. A very different woman I'm told."

"Over there."

The bartender pointed toward a small Asian standing beside a door leading to one of the back rooms. "Tell him what you want."

"Thanks, pal."

The whiskey-fortified patron walked over to the man by the door. "I'm looking for Ariana. I got money. How much?"

"Fifty dollars, American."

"Okay. You're on."

He reached in his pocket and pulled out the money, dropping most of it as he handed it to the pimp. "Sorry pal. I'm a little drunk. Where do I find her?"

"Just inside here. First door to the right. You got thirty minutes. Get it done or your time is up."

"Got it."

He entered the dimly lit room, not much bigger than a closet to see a woman sitting upright on the bed. Even with the scant light, he could see she was tall and slim with long hair down to her shoulders. She was bony and unusually structured. Of course, most tranny prostitutes could never get past their male beginnings and this one was no exception. He walked over to her and she leaned forward toward him, grabbing his belt buckle and pulling him closer. It was good that the light in the room was so dim. It helped to hide the needle tracks which covered most of her arms and legs. Her eyes were only half open and when she opened her mouth to accept his member, he would have seen that it was devoid of teeth or tongue. But, he was not there for small talk. Ariana understood what he wanted and was only too willing to give it to him. If she provided him with the satisfaction he needed, then her pimp would provide her with what she needed later that evening. She had no reservations as to what she must do to survive. For her there was no other world and there never would be. Aaron Goldman was deeply entrenched in his new life as a whore and would not be as lucky as Alicia. There would be no Mary Lou to help him.

* * *

Ernest Pearlman was not a happy man. He thought he had struck a deal with Delores that would allow him to take control of Virginia Industrial. She had betrayed that trust and left him hung out to dry. With Alicia and Delores working as a team, they had a huge majority of the stock. Now that Delores had been selected as Chairman of the Board, what he thought meant nothing. He had sold all his stock and was certain that Angus McVeigh was fronting for the sisters when he had made the purchase.

His emasculation by the sisters had been more than he could take. Money was not the issue. He had more than he could spend in ten lifetimes. He needed revenge. He would find a way to ruin them all. Then, he might just buy the company outright and reclaim his pride. He had spent a great deal of his life plotting business maneuvers and vanquishing his opponents with the help of corrupt bankers, brokers, and attorneys. The one attorney he thought to be the most capable, Fred Burns, was no longer available. The word on the street was that he had stolen a great sum of money from one of his clients, presumably Aaron Goldman, and had left the country.

It was even rumored that Aaron may have fallen prey to Burns when he confronted him with the theft. Aaron's abandoned car and a suicide note was found a short time later alongside the banks of the Chesapeake Bay. The note indicated he could no longer live with his own infidelity to his estranged wife and that he had been swindled by a close friend out of a ton of cash. The authorities were not very sympathetic and had not found another, more plausible reason for his disappearance. Nonetheless, Pearlman needed a contact and all he had was a name on the back of a business card Burns had given him. Literally, out of ideas and full of hate and whiskey, he placed a call to that number.

"May I help you?" the voice responded without giving any other information as to who was answering the call.

"My name is Pearlman. I got your number from an attorney I knew, Fred Burns. Haven't seen him in quite some time but he thought you could help me."

"Yes, I do remember that he mentioned your name at one time. Said you might just give me a call. What can I do for you, Mr. Pearlman?"

"I have been screwed by a business associate. It wasn't just a business deal gone south; it was a butch dyke broad who delighted in ridiculing me all over the business community. She made me look like an idiot. I can't let that stand. I need someone to help me set the matter straight. Give it back to her. Is this something you can help with?"

"I suppose I could. But my services are very special. Discretion is everything and I'm not inexpensive."

"I've got money. That's not an issue. Where can I meet with you?"

"You know where the old Jefferson Hotel is downtown?"

"Of course."

"Six o'clock tomorrow night. Drive to the alley around back. I'll be waiting there for you. Just park the car. Come by yourself and bring me a manila envelope with two hundred grand in it. When I'm finished taking care of the details of this job to your complete satisfaction I'll want the other half."

"You weren't kidding about being pricey, were you?"

"You could handle this by yourself."

"Like I said, price is not the issue. I'll be there."

* * *

A light rain was falling as Ernest Pearlman pulled into the alley behind the Jefferson Hotel. He could see no one there but he wanted this to happen so he decided to wait and see who showed up. After ten or fifteen minutes a man in a long dark raincoat knocked on the passenger side door.

"It's not locked. Get in."

Doctor K hopped in the front with Pearlman.

"Okay, what's next?"

"Pull back out to the interstate headed south. I'll tell you which exit to take. You brought the money with you?"

Pearlman patted an envelope sitting next to him on the front seat.

"May I open it?"

"Don't trust me, eh?"

"I have found in my lifetime that to trust anyone is incredibly foolish. Is there anyone you trust who hasn't let you down?"

"Now that you mention it, no. Why should I trust you?"

"You shouldn't. You should trust that I want the other half of this money. Mind if I open the envelope and do a rough count?"

"Help yourself."

"Fine. Just keep heading south. I'll let you know where to turn."

Doctor K just kept silent as he counted the money. Satisfied it was correct, he tucked it under his raincoat in the inside pocket. A few minutes later he started to give Pearlman instructions.

"Okay, take the next exit."

"There's nothing down here but the old Richmond docks. They don't even use them anymore. The road is probably shit."

"Just turn."

A few minutes down the road, he had Pearlman turn off into an old warehouse that once stored tobacco leaving Virginia by ship.

"Pull in right here. I'll open that old garage door."

Doctor K disappeared into the building; a dim light came on inside and the door opened. Pearlman pulled the car inside. He was beginning to get a little nervous in the desolate surroundings. He really knew nothing about this guy other than Burns had recommended him. He parked the car in the filthy storage area of the building and followed Doctor K to a small door off to the side.

"Where the hell are you taking me?"

"Surely you didn't think these affairs would be conducted downtown in an office tower?"

"I guess not. But this is a nasty old building."

"Not the part where I conduct my affairs. Just follow me."

The men came to a steel door at the end of a short hall. Doctor K opened it and motioned for Pearlman to follow him. As he entered he cut on a small light in the corner which didn't cast much more than a soft glow on what looked like it may have been used as an office of sorts. There was one long rectangular table in the center that was on wheels and covered with a white sheet.

"What's this all about? Looks like one of those carts they put people on before they load them into an ambulance."

"Precisely. I can buy them very inexpensively at medical surplus sales when old hospitals are being torn down. They make wonderful work tables. I especially like the fact that they are completely stainless steel. Very easy to clean. Fingerprints don't work well in my line of work."

"I would imagine not. What exactly is it that you do? Other than cause people problems."

"I'm especially good at relieving stress."

"Whose stress?"

Just as he answered Pearlman's question he stuck a hypodermic into his neck in one swift motion. Pearlman grabbed at the pain, looked at Doctor K and within ten seconds slumped over onto the gurney. Doctor K smiled as he pushed Pearlman's frame totally onto the table. "Mine. Who else?"

Ernest Pearlman woke up staring into a bright light hanging overhead. He started to sit up only to find that he was securely strapped onto the stainless table. He also realized he was completely naked and quite chilled.

"Doctor K, or whatever your name is, what's going on here? What the hell are you doing?"

Doctor K walked over beside him. "Well, that didn't take very long. You've been out less than an hour. I was hoping I wouldn't have to hang around here all evening. I have a lot on my plate right now."

"What the hell are you talking about? You took my money. You're working for me."

"Not exactly, Ernest. May I call you Ernest?"

"No, you may not. Now let me up from here. Now. I'm not fucking around with you. You'll be in so much trouble you'll never find an end to it."

"Please, don't be so dramatic. Here, let me help you."

Doctor K took off a strip of duct tape and pushed it down over Pearlman's mouth. "There, now you can rest a while so I can get everything prepared and in place. Now, let's see. Oh yes, Fred. I need to bring Fred in here."

Doctor K opened a closet door revealing poor old Fred Burns, strapped securely in a wheelchair. He got behind him and pushed the chair over next to the gurney beside Pearlman.

"Let's be honest with one another, Fred. I don't think you're really enjoying your life all that much anymore. No BMWs, no fine clothes, no fancy restaurants, no women. I think you've probably paid enough penance to satisfy everyone involved. I am very proud of you though. I think you were one of my finest efforts. You and Aaron. Oh yes, did I tell you Aaron has a new job over in the Far East? Doing quite well, I understand. Now let's see here. I really don't have much time or interest in doing things to you that you're too dumb to understand anymore. Actually, it might be fun. Kind of like plucking the wings off flies, but I digress. I just need to go ahead and finish you so I can take care of our friend here, Ernest Pearlman."

Pearlman was straining his head as high off the gurney as he could to see what was going on. He could barely believe what he was witnessing. There in front of him was a cartoon version of Fred Burns, legless in a wheelchair and smiling like a baboon while he watched Doctor K move about the room.

"Ah, Ernest. I see you are interested in what's going on here. I think that's perfectly appropriate as you are going to get credit for it."

Pearlman's eyes were as wide as saucers as he watched Doctor
K. First he took a large, industrial size extension cord and unfurled
it from its coil. Next, he cut the female plug from the end and
stripped the wires of their insulation. He bared about three inches
of both the positive and negative wires. He then walked over to
Burns and wrapped one wire around each of his ears. Burns
giggled at the feeling as the wires were tightened. As an
afterthought, Doctor K went over to Pearlman and stuffed his
overcoat under his head so he could see easier without having to
strain to hold his head up.

"Ernest, this isn't going to take nearly as long as I like for these
things to last but, like I said, I'm kind of in a hurry this evening.
Now, keep looking at Fred's face if you will. I'm just going to go
over here and plug him in. Very exciting stuff."

As Doctor K plugged in the hot end of the electric chord to the
receptacle, Pearlman stared at Fred Burn's face. There was an
immediate jerking of his entire body. He flung his head back into
the chair so hard an audible pop could be heard in the room.
Doctor K moved over almost directly in front of Burns and
watched the effects with intense interest. In less than fifteen
seconds, smoke began to pour from around Burn's ears and finally
from his eye sockets. Doctor K left the chord plugged in until
Burns' head began to look like an overcooked marshmallow in a
campfire. The smell was sickening. Pearlman was now sobbing
intensely with his eyes shut. He wanted to see no more. Finally,
Doctor K unplugged the chord and pulled the loose ends away
from Burns' body.

"Most interesting. I've never done that before. You ever see
anyone electrocuted like that, Ernest? I couldn't really tell how
painful it was to Burns as his diminished mental faculties certainly

made it a lot easier on him. Well, good for him. He won't have to sell pencils on the street corner anymore. Now, Ernest. You're up."

Pearlman struggled as hard as he possibly could against his restraints. He knew whatever this maniac had in mind was going to be horrific and he would rather him just kill him quickly. His instincts told him that was not what Doctor K had in mind.

"Now, Ernest. I know you're interested in what I have in mind so I'll just tell you enough that you won't have to worry yourself sick about what's going on right now. Killing people is not what I normally want to be doing. People die and that's that. Once they're gone, they feel nothing; they know nothing. That's certainly no fun for me. I want to sustain their lives as long as I possibly can. I love to see the fear in a person's eyes, much like what I see in yours at this moment. That's the gratification I'm looking for. Pain is the ultimate human experience. How many times have you heard someone say, they don't mind dying, they just don't want to suffer, to linger. They fear the pain associated with dying more than dying itself. It is the peak of life, supreme pain at the threshold of death. I like to be there, to watch and, even more, to be the creator of the moment. It's at that precise moment that I get the most incredible rush of power a person can possibly imagine. I think I said that very well.

"Oh yes, getting back to why you're here. To tell you the truth, Ernest, this Virginia Industrial mess is just that, a real mess. It seems that everyone running the company is just plain bad. You, Aaron, Fred, Delores, Enright, all genuinely awful people. You don't care what you do to anyone as long as you win. And of course, there are the innocent players like Alicia, Mary Lou, and even sweet little Chelsea. I would never hurt a child. At least, I don't think I would. I'll admit I've thought about it but it's something I don't really have a firm grasp on right now.

"So, a lot of people have been hurt here. The police are looking for someone to blame and we need to furnish them with that. People need closure. So, that's what you are. You are their closure. That should make you feel somewhat better that you're bringing a sense of relief and justice into a world so full of frightened people yearning for just that. When they find your charred remains they'll quickly determine that you had tortured and finally killed poor old Fred Burns and unfortunately electrocuted yourself in the process.

"A personal ledger will be found in your belongings documenting to the world your hideous actions that resulted in all the mayhem to the other folks over at Virginia Industrial. It will all make sense, as you hated Aaron Burns. He was your enemy. You took out his closest confidant, Burns, his wife Diane, and tried to hang Alicia's abduction on Aaron as well. There's even a few other surprises in it for everyone but I think you get the picture now.

"Unfortunately, I can't tie the electric cord around your ears like I did with Burns. That would never fly as an accident. No, I think a simple connection to one of your hands will do just fine. I would like more but I can't take the chance of messing up the crime scene. I'm considered somewhat of an expert by those in the know. So, you're all hooked up now, Ernest. Tell you what, if you want to do one kind thing on your way out, how about fighting this as long as you can. If I have to go to all this trouble, the least you can do is give me a little rush from it. So, here we go."

The lights flickered twice and the familiar smell came back into the room.

18

"Henrico Country 911. What's the nature of your emergency?"

"Yes, ma'am. I'm calling from the office of Mr. Ernest Pearlman. I'm his secretary. He left me a note this morning saying to call 911 if I couldn't reach him. I've tried his cell phone a dozen times but I can't get him to answer. It just goes to voicemail. He's never done anything like this and I've worked for him for over twenty years."

"Yes, ma'am. Do you have any reason to think he might be in danger?"

"I don't know what to think. Like I said, he's overdue for appointments here and he left this weird note."

"Can you give me his cell phone number? Perhaps we can locate him that way."

"Yes, here it is."

* * *

"Aubrey?"

"Yes, is that you, Freda?"

"That's right, Aubrey. Listen, I'm out at an abandoned warehouse near Chesterfield County. It's the old Richmond Dock exit off 95 South. You know where I'm talking about?"

"Sure. What's up?"

"I think you're going to want to see this. I'm at a crime scene. We traced a guy name Ernest Pearlman's cell phone number to this old warehouse and well, we found two bodies. One has been butchered and then electrocuted and the other looks like he accidently executed himself while murdering the first guy. And guess what? They're both connected to Alicia and Aaron Goldman. You remember, Virginia Industrial."

"How could I forget. Okay, I'll put some pants on and I'll get there as quickly as I can."

Freda Payne continued to examine the murder scene. It was certainly as gruesome as anything she'd ever seen. It had a ring of familiarity to it though. She just couldn't put her finger on it. Within the hour Aubrey showed up, looking like he'd been roused from a deep sleep.

"Okay, Freda, what do we have here?"

"You tell me. Fred Burns was Aaron Goldman's attorney. We all thought he'd absconded with a lot of the Goldman's money after doing away with Aaron. That's obviously incorrect since his corpse is laying here with no legs and his head almost burned off his body with electricity. And over here, this guy was Ernest Pearlman, a prime contender for Chairman of the Board of Goldman's company up until recently. There was a lot of bad blood there."

"How did you find the bodies?"

"Pearlman's secretary called. Said she couldn't get up with her boss and that he'd left a note telling her to call 911 if she couldn't get up with him."

"That's rather odd. Seems like he suspected something might happen to him."

"There's just so much about all of this that doesn't make sense. And, doesn't this crime scene seem familiar to you?"

"Absolutely. It's almost a copy of what we found in that neighbor's basement with the little kidnapped girl. What was her name? Chelsea?"

"That's it, Aubrey. Could it be the same guy? Could Pearlman have been the one we've been looking for all along?"

"He certainly doesn't match the neighbor's description of the elderly, quiet gentleman that lived next to the Josephs."

"I know. It all just doesn't add up yet. Does it?"

"I'm sure all the pieces are here, Freda. We just have to reassemble the puzzle."

"If anybody can do it, Aubrey, it's you. I'm sure of that."

"I will give it my best effort."

                              * * *

It was late on Friday evening and Freda was ready to go home. She had just one meeting left. Aubrey had called early and asked if he could come by. "Come on in, Aubrey; the door's open. What are you up to? Can I get you a coffee?"

"That sounds great, Freda."

They made small talk for a couple of minutes while each added sugar and cream to their coffees. Aubrey took a couple of sips before he sat down. "Freda, I think I have this whole thing worked out with regards to the Goldmans and the rest of the sordid crew at his company."

"You do? That would be wonderful. At this point, I don't know who to blame for what. I mean almost everyone over there is dead."

"There, you laid your finger right on it and skipped right past the obvious."

"What are you getting at?"

"Who is the last person standing? Who wins in all of this?"

"I guess the only one left to gain from any of this would be Delores Thompson, Alicia's sister."

"Bingo. She's so obvious it's easy to overlook her trying to solve something and making it too complicated at the same time."

"How do you connect the dots back to her?"

"Okay, bear with me now and I'll try to walk you through all of this."

"I'm all ears." Freda sat back behind her desk and listened intently while Aubrey laid out the case.

"Okay. Who was the first person to be a casualty in this drama?"

"Alicia?"

"Nope, Enright. Remember the horrible boat accident?"

"That's right. Not an accident, huh?"

"Not at all. You'll notice that whenever there's been a cause of death other than an obvious murder, the body has always been so deteriorated that it was impossible to assume anything other than the obvious. In his case, a boating accident. A horrible gas explosion that blew him into small pieces and even charred them beyond recognition. Had to use DNA to identify him, couldn't even find an intact section of jawbone to examine dental records. And he was in charge of the books at the company. If anybody was playing games with the cash, he would be the first to find out."

"So far so good. That makes sense. Go on."

"Next we have poor Alicia. Abducted, subject to God knows what kinds of insane torture, forced into addiction and even prostitution. So far removed from her past that finding her was just a pure stroke of luck. Bad luck for her in one way and fortunate in another. I understand she's getting along much better but still hasn't been able to reconstruct what happened to her or anything about her kidnapper. Of course, her disappearance made her poor suffering husband look like a martyr up until he got caught with his cute little girlfriend and Pearlman tried to paint him as a greedy jerk so he could oust him from the Chairmanship.

"Then, there are the rumors that Aaron's attorney had stolen a bunch of money from him and gone on the lamb. Only now, we know that isn't so. We found his burned body just a couple of weeks ago, long after everyone assumed he had killed Aaron and tried to make it look like a suicide. Of course, no body has been found to confirm his death. But, we know he's not running the family business and that would have been his main concern based on everything we know about him. If he were still alive, that's where he would be. And then, the near breakthrough with that little girl, Chelsea that showed us someone else was involved in all of this, someone with a great interest in torturing and in sick methods of taking his victims lives. Enter this recent accident with Pearlman that clearly connected him with those laboratory types of killings. Obvious, huh? But not really. He would never have left a note for his secretary to call 911 if she couldn't get up with him. It took you less than an hour to find him once you had his cell phone number. So, that leaves just one person standing who has anything to gain from all these other people and to my mind that's Delores Thompson, new Chairman of Virginia Industrial. I'm willing to bet that if you do a little investigation with the help of the SEC you will find recent large stock transactions between Miss Thompson and most of the other parties who are now in the next world. Of course, her somewhat mentally impaired sister now lets her control all her stock and voila, there's no need for Aaron Goldman. He's really just in the way at that point. Everyone with any knowledge of what actually transpired is dead. I do suspect that somewhere out there is a hired gun, probably long gone by now who did her dirty work, who handled these crimes in a very professional way. So much so that we don't really have any proof at all, other than the final beneficiary, and that's Miss Thompson. I think turning this over to the SEC might be the best course of action at this point."

"That certainly looks incriminating, Aubrey. You paint a very convincing picture."

"At least, that's my best guess of what has occurred here. I'm willing to bet that Miss Delores Thompson is in this up to her eyeballs. Perhaps she'll crack under some intense pressure from the feds."

"You may be right, Aubrey. You may just have solved all of this. What a sick affair."

"There is no limit to just how far a person will go to get what they want. If I've learned anything in my thirty years in this business, it's that there is no bottom to depravity."

19

The Police Benevolent Association's annual ball and award presentation was one of the most elaborate events Richmond hosted to bring in the New Year. Members of the Richmond Police Department and the Henrico County Sheriff's Office rewarded individual officers and staff for exceptional performance. These awards usually went to officers who placed themselves in the line of fire to protect or defend the citizens they worked for. This year, Freda Payne was the key presenter for the Police Department.

"Good evening to you all. I am truly honored to be tonight's presenter for several reasons. First, as a longtime member of this department, I know the countless hours and personal sacrifices many officers bring to the job. The pay is low, the stress is high, and the danger always present. This is a job most do because they feel called to it and can't imagine themselves doing anything else. I know these men and women personally.

"Second, tonight's recipient is a gentleman I've had the privilege of working with for many years. Today, though retired, he always comes through when we call him. He offers his time and talents to help us solve cases, many of which have gone unsolved for years before he put his expertise to work for us. He is truly an expert in his field and Richmond is fortunate to have him here to call on. This is the first time we have ever given the prestigious Meritorious Service Award to someone not an active member of the force. Particularly in this past year, there really was no one more deserving. He solved four murders related to the incidents at Virginia Industrial and found twelve-year-old Chelsea Joseph unharmed after being abducted by a serial killer. I've seen him in action and I'm glad to say he's on our team. This year's winner is, Mr. Aubrey Pryor. Please come forward Aubrey."

The audience knew Aubrey's track record well and gave him the standing ovation. Being a shy individual, Aubrey declined to make any lengthy remarks and merely thanked the officers and the selection committee for the high honor. He then humbly returned to his seat. He left early and spoke only to say thank you to those who recognized him as he left. Though honored and extremely pleased with himself, there was still one loose end he needed to secure before his mind could consider the job complete.

* * *

Delores and Alicia were up late in the magnificent sitting room of Delores' Monument Avenue home. They were extremely pleased with the recent events in their lives. Delores was now in full control of Virginia Industrial. Alicia was getting stronger and more confident every day. She was also in love, though it was now with another woman, Carolyn. Her life had gone down a very dark and violent road but she had found her way back to her old world. In many ways her life was fuller than before. She was now her own woman, healthy, stronger and more appreciative of every day. There was also something very noticeable going on in her mind.

"Delores, did you buy that painting over there from Furman's? I think I remember when you got it."

"I did. It's a Picasso from his blue period. He was a young portrait painter in Paris when he created that wonderful piece. You say you remember me winning it at Furman's?"

"Yes, I remember clearly. Many things are starting to come back to me. I'm so happy to be able to recall things from my past. I thought they were lost forever. I think I will soon be whole again. Did Carolyn call today?"

"Yes dear. She's still at her folks' home in Colorado and said she was having such a good visit she wouldn't be back until the weekend. I told her we were fine here, to have fun. Let's drink a toast to our futures, darling. To wonderful memories, both those already here and those still to be made."

"To memories!"

The two women stayed up until after midnight small talking and discussing trips planned for the coming year. Shortly before one a.m. they both retired to their rooms. Delores' room could have easily been moved, untouched, from a great English castle. Mammoth in size with gold leaf wallpaper and Louis XIV furnishings, there was more opulence and wealth in her bedroom than in the entire population of most small cities. She liked the feeling of power and stature it gave her to live in such surroundings. She set her champagne glass by her nightstand, removed her floor length silk robe and slid under the satin sheets of her king-sized antique bed. It was late. She was tired and soon fell off into a very deep sleep. Feeling movement against her face she awoke to swat away what felt like a feather teasing her forehead. After several hand brushes pursuing the tickle to her face, she awoke feeling a presence in the room. She rubbed her eyes to remove the dried crust that wanted to hold her eyelids together. As the blurred vision of the dark room began to clear, she could clearly make out the shadow of an individual standing beside her.

"Alicia, what is it?"

"Wrong. Alicia is sleeping like a baby in her own room. It's just me."

"Aubrey? How did you get in here?"

"Oh, come on Delores. I've been in police work all my life. You think this would really be a challenge? When we talked before, you left your keys on the desk in your foyer. A very common practice. A little modeling clay in my pocket and voila! Five seconds later I have a perfect impression of your house key and yes, even your Bentley key. Of course, since you always use Evan, your driver, I never really understood why you keep a key for the car with you."

"What are you doing here, in my room, in the middle of the night?"

"A really great question, Delores. Before I answer that though, take a look over at your window there."

Delores turned her head to look to the window on the far side of the room. As she did she felt a quick twinge on her arm and turned to see Aubrey holding an empty syringe in his hand.

"That went really quick. Almost didn't feel it, did you?"

"What have you done to me? What was in that needle?"

"You will be dead in less than ten minutes unless you do exactly as I tell you. I've given you a very heavy dose of a combination of two very potent drugs. Kind of my own invention, I'm proud to say. Now, let's not waste any more valuable time, shall we? I've taken the liberty to draw up a little note here that I need you to sign. It's a Power of Attorney that I'll need in order to vote your stock."

Delores looked at the sheet of paper but the letters were already blurred and she could tell her vision was being affected by the drugs he had just injected. "I'm not signing anything. I can't even read this."

"Suit yourself. I'm sure you'd rather be dead than give up any sort of power. I do admire you so much though, Delores. Of all the degenerates that have sat at the top of Virginia Industrial, you were the worst, or the best, depending on your point of view. No one will ever know that it was you that hooked me up with Fred Burns and had him propose the Alicia abduction. That little adventure wound up steering all the guilt toward Alicia's husband and even explained the death of Fred Burns and Mr. Enright. You are, in many respects, a criminal mastermind. In that regard, I personally admire your abilities. At times you are absolutely brilliant. But, enough fawning over you. You really need to sign this sheet of paper and then I'll be more than happy to hand you the antidote. You'll never be quite the same, but you will be alive."

"What... What's happening to my head? I'm swimming, can't think..."

"Just sign the paper, dear, right here so I can help you. Yes, that's it. A really nice signature. Perfect." I'll be leaving you now."

"What about the anti... Goat?... The ampy... The...?"

"The antidote? I'm sorry, darling. I didn't think to bring it. And besides, I now have what I need."

Aubrey Pryor, a/k/a Doctor K, a/k/a Kale Spencer, muttered to himself before leaving, "And now, all the loose ends are tied. Poor Delores, no longer able to live with her guilt, leaves a confession and takes her own life with a massive overdose. These rich people. Just can't leave well enough alone."

As Doctor K turned to leave the room, he literally jumped backward as he saw Alicia standing in the doorway. "You startled me, Alicia. You remember me. I'm Aubrey Pryor."

"I remember exactly who you are. You are Doctor K. You are the man who tortured me and ruined my life."

"Okay, I'll accept that. I deserved it. But how much did you just hear? Did you hear that your sister is who arranged for you to be abducted? She never wanted you to survive that. And though you did, she still used those events toward her own ends. I'm just the hired hand you might say."

Doctor K reached toward the inside of his jacket as though reaching for a weapon. As he looked up, now with a gun in his hand, the doorway was empty.

"Alicia? Alicia darling. No need to make this hard on yourself. You know how creative I can be. You can go peacefully into that dark night or maybe not so quick and painless. This is totally your call, sweetie."

Doctor K followed her out into the hallway. It was very dark with only a small amount of light radiating from a table lamp downstairs. The staircase connecting the four floors of the mammoth brownstone was open with two landings and allowed an internal view up or down. The farther up the stairs however, the less light could be found. Aubrey started up the dark stairs, moving stealthily and listening for Alicia's footsteps or breathing. As he reached the top stair of the fourth floor landing he could clearly see Alicia's silhouette standing in the doorway.

"Now Alicia, don't be afraid. I'm on your side. Your sister was evil. She was the one who wanted you out of the way. She ruined your life. She did away with your husband Aaron. You should see what happened to him. Just awful. But I always liked you and would never hurt you, never. Now, don't move. Just stay right there and I'll help you back to the bed. You won't feel a thing. Not a thing."

Alicia stared him right in the eye as she replied, "I'm sure you don't want me to feel a thing. But that's not how I feel about you. I want you to feel it all."

Doctor K, walked purposely closer to Alicia, pistol in hand. "I'm sorry you want it this way. But I understand. We'll do this your way."

Just as he raised his arm to take point blank aim at Alicia, a falling Delores grabbed for the arm holding the pistol. At that same instant, Alicia lunged forward plunging a razor sharp butcher knife blade deep into his gut. The pistol fell from his hand hitting numerous steps as it cascaded down the steep staircase. He stared with an unbelieving look into Alicia's face. "You, you... Agnes... You..."

As she scowled at him with a look of eternal hate she put her second hand onto the handle of the knife and twisted with all the strength in her body. "I'm not Agnes. I'm Alicia and this is for what you did to me..."

She used all her might to twist the knife blade and run the entire width of his abdominal cavity. Doctor K groaned the unmistakable sounds of death. Alicia made one more pronouncement, "And that was for Mary Lou, you worthless bastard. Time for you to go to hell!"

Doctor K fell in a limp pile onto the floor in front of her, his cries growing weaker until there was only silence emanating from him. Delores now barely able to stand, and needing immediate medical attention drug her way over to her sister. "Alicia, get help. He drugged me. I can barely see. I need help quickly."

Alicia went to her sister and grabbed her firmly by her shoulders. She stared intently into her now half-shut eyes. "You were wrong about me, Delores. I'm not weak. I'm strong, much stronger than you. I don't need anyone else to do my killing for me."

With a fire inside needing to grab for all the fuel it could find to grow, she pushed forward until Delores fell backward and then down two flights of stairs before she came to a dead stop on the second floor landing of the staircase. Alicia walked down to where her sister lay on the steps. She was barely breathing and staring up at the ceiling. Alicia knelt by her side. Delores struggled to speak, spitting up blood between words. "I can't, can't feel my arms or legs. Can't breathe. I'm dying. I'm sorry, Alicia. Sorry for everything."

"I know, I know. But don't try to talk. I called for help. You're going to make it. You're going to live. And I'm going to take care of you. Alicia is going to do whatever you need. I'm going to look out for you. Just like you've looked out for me."

Alicia paused and added one last sentence, more for herself than her sister. "Exactly like you took care of me."

The sound of a siren screaming through the otherwise still night could be heard.

20

Palm trees on the shoreline swayed with the warm tropical breeze. The sun was just setting over the spectacular Caribbean islands. The sky was an incredible burnt orange and it radiated off the surface of the pristine aqua water which was as clear as the air above it. It was an extraordinarily beautiful evening in a place known for its beautiful sunsets. The gleaming white, two hundred foot plus power yacht *Superlative* was anchored in thirty feet of water less than a hundred yards from the pink sand beach. The recessed deck lights reflected off the stainless steel and glass structures forming the main salon of this magnificent creation.

"Well, my dear. Is it all I told you it would be?"

Joan Williams, a terrycloth robe covering her otherwise nude body walked over to the gentleman and bent down from behind him. He could feel her warm breasts on the back of his head as she gently stroked his scalp. She bent down even more and embraced his neck tightly before kissing his forehead and then releasing him. She walked over to a chaise lounge directly in front of his. A uniformed steward came by with a tray and offered her a drink. "Champagne, ma'am?"

"Of course. Thank you, young man." She smiled at the tanned and muscled twenty-year-old as he pushed the tray close enough to her for her to grasp the crystal goblet. He smiled back.

"Yes, ma'am. You're very welcome."

The much older gentleman now seated directly in front of her took a deep drag from a twenty-dollar Cuban cigar as he spoke. "So Joan, are you enjoying yourself? I told you we were the perfect team. Together, we can't be stopped. You could say, the world is our oyster. You will never have to worry about paying a bill, buying nice clothes and presents for yourself, or where the money is coming from to grow old, beautiful lady. You stick with me, take care of my needs, and every woman in the world will envy you. You have it all."

"Can I get you a drink, my darling? You have to be dehydrated after I helped drain you of all your bodily fluids this afternoon."

"That was very special, my darling. You make me feel like I'm twenty years old again. Not bad for sixty-five, eh?"

Joan, with her back to older man opened a small vial she had carried with her in the pocket of her robe. She emptied the contents into the glass of sparkling Perrier."

"Here, my love. Drink this. Then, you know what I'd like to do?"

"Anything. You name it."

"I'd like for us to go swimming. How about skinny dipping off the stern? Just me and you and the delicious warm ocean. Besides, your trunks would just get in the way of my hands, if you understand my meaning. I just can't get enough of your manhood. You are my huge, hairy beast. You are the perfect man for me."

Angus McVeigh, completely full of his success in all things, downed the deadly liquid in two swallows. He quickly pulled his bathing trunks off to reveal a torso hairier than a silverback at the state zoo. He crossed over to Joan Williams and kissed her squarely on the mouth, driving his tongue deep into her throat. He pulled away, walked down the staircase leading from the stern of his yacht to the swim platform which rested just off the surface of the water. He yelled back to Joan as he watched her take off her robe revealing the magnificent body he craved beyond his imagination.

"Hurry darling, let's have our fun. I'm starting to feel a little tired."

"I know, Angus. I know. I'll be right there, my love."

Under her breath she said to herself, "My fun is just getting ready to start."

* * *

The highly burnished conference table at Virginia Industrial was covered with papers, manila folders, and empty water bottles. There was a lot of hand shaking, smiling, and back slapping in progress. Alicia, standing at the end of the table, was wearing a tight-fitting tailored business suit and looking every bit the most powerful person in the room. She looked over at her lover Carolyn and gave her a knowing smile. There was only one other woman in the room. In a far corner, near the large, panoramic window sat Delores. She was in a multifaceted wheelchair. There were braces holding her in place; even a supportive collar holding her head upright. She had an oxygen nosepiece leading from her nostrils to the battery driven tank of oxygen on a small platform on the back of the chair. Behind her stood a uniformed nurse. Reacting to a gurgling sound from Delores, she reached down and straightened the nosepiece. She then took her hand and gently brushed several strands of hair from in front of her eyes. Delores gurgled a little louder causing a few of those in the room to turn and look at her. The nurse knelt beside her, looked her in the face, and then placed her finger on her lips and quietly said, "Shhhhh. Don't want to disturb the meeting, sweetie. They have important business to talk about."

If there ever was a look that completely spelled despair, it was on Delores' face.

Her little sister addressed the group. "Gentlemen, gentlemen. I can't tell you how great it's been knowing and working with you all this past month. I know it's been a difficult time here at VI but I feel confident that everything is now in the best shape it has been in for the past decade. I want to thank you all for accepting my offer to purchase back your shares so that I could fulfill my father's wishes for the company to be under the control of the family who built it. You should all be very pleased knowing that you received double the market price for your stock and you can now look your golden years in the face with a smile. So, as we leave here today, we will be shutting the door on a very frustrating chapter in all our lives and saying welcome to a very bright tomorrow. Thank you all for coming. Carolyn, let's leave these gentlemen to toast their success."

Alicia looked over at the nurse and motioned with her hand that it was time to push Delores out to her waiting handicap van which stood ready in the circle drive out front. The ramp was down and there were two young orderlies in white jackets ready to help Delores. Alicia and Carolyn walked down the hall, through the polished marble and stainless steel lobby out to the waiting Rolls. The driver stood beside the back door and smartly opened it as the two women approached. In only a moment, the limousine disappeared down the cedar-lined private drive. Shortly afterward, the handicap van followed the same path out of Virginia Industrial.

photograph by Robert Dumon Photography

About the Author

Les Pendleton lives in historic New Bern, North Carolina. His writing style conveys the influence of his career in motion pictures. Many people share their impression that reading his novels feels as if you are watching the characters come to life on the silver screen. Actual locations in coastal North Carolina are featured in many of his books. His writing spans a wide array of genres from action adventure, romance, historical fiction, suspense-filled mysteries and autobiographies. Les spends every free moment with his family and friends sailing in Pamlico Sound and the Atlantic Coast.

For more about the author, visit **www.lespendleton.com**

* * *

Thank you for reading this novel.
We invite you to share your thoughts and reactions
by going to Amazon.com/author/lespendleton
and posting a review.

Essie Press

Made in the USA
Columbia, SC
24 July 2021

42133821R00148